A Crucifixion In Mexico

A Crucifixion In Mexico

Kathleen Walker

Black Heron Press
Post Office Box 95676
Seattle, Washington 98145
http://mav.net/blackheron

ISBN 0-930773-52-7

Cover art by Michael Contreras

Published by
     Black Heron Press
     Post Office Box 95676
     Seattle, Washington 98145
     http://mav.net/blackheron

For the little Virgin with
the broken hand

Gloria

1

I saw a crucifixion once. I don't tell the story often. It is too hard to start and once started you have to go all the way to the end. Then you have to look at the faces of those you've told and see what they think of you, not of the story, but of you. I hate myself for that, telling the story to people I hardly know so they will know something about me.

I did see a crucifixion once. I saw a man hung on a cross, hammered to it, hung until dead, which wasn't all that long a time. It was supposed to be longer.

Someone once told me I should write it down, the story of that day, but I can't. Twenty years later and I still can't write about it. I can hardly talk about it. I've only told the story three times without Andrew and that was three times too many. With Andrew, I have told it another three times.

Andrew was there that day and he is the one who begins the story when we are together. I always know when he will begin. We will be holding our first drinks of the night, margaritas, always in thick stubby glasses, not those green bowl things you get in Mexican restaurants. We are always in his parents' house in Sedona, Arizona, home of the rich and the not-so-great artists, his father being one of them. I sit on the couch or on the fat leather ottoman. Andrew sits next to me or near me and whoever it is who is about to be introduced to our common history sits across from us.

Before he starts, he always gives me this little smile, as though he is saying, "It is time now, Gloria, to tell the story." Then he turns to the guest.

"You know, we once saw a crucifixion. Yes, we did. In Mexico," he says each time. I nod and it begins again.

*

The reaction to that opening line is always interesting and always the same.

"You're kidding," they say. "You have to be kidding, right?"

They are the women Andrew has brought home to his parents and to me. He has never asked my opinion of them afterward and I've never offered one. I think this is his idea of a baptism by fire. If they can make it past this, past the weekend in the strangeness of Sedona with all its ticky-tacky stores, past his parents, that rabid Republican father of his, past the drinking, past me and past the crucifixion story, they can make it through anything. That may be his thinking.

Or, he could be just trying to reveal something of himself, some depth or whatever it is the softer men feel they are supposed to show and that this story is the only way he knows how to do it. I've never asked him why he tells the story and none of the women has lasted much longer than the weekend, as far as I can figure. So, perhaps the story doesn't work well for Andrew or maybe it works too well.

The other thing the listeners always say is, "Oh, you mean one of those passion plays, like in Germany? Is that what you mean?" They are happy with that thought. But we shake our heads slowly, tighten our jaws to show how much more serious our story is than that little drama.

No, this is nothing like that, no cute folk with leather shorts and hairy knees climbing mountains and singing songs. Nothing like a happy passion play in Bavaria or wherever it is where lovers of all things living and growing and haters of all dead Jews gather. No, our crucifixion was nothing like that.

Yet, that is how it started. I did think we were going to see a passion play, all innocent and clean. I had organized the day, an adventure. I told them how interesting it would be. I'm the one who got them there to the taco stands and the priests in their pink petticoats and to the one poor man who was about to be crucified. That's the way I remember it and I remember things quite well.

The first thing they always want to know is why. They want that answer before they have heard the story about all the things that happened that day. Why, they want to know, was a man crucified? Why is something we Americans always want to know first.

A Mexican wouldn't ask why. A Mexican would nod us on, agreeing that yes, men are crucified, and wait to hear the story. A Frenchman would shrug and make that little kissing movement with his lips, a moué, a sort of "Oh, well, I've heard it all, even that, but I will listen." But, Americans, they have to have the reason first.

"A penance," Andrew tells them and then it is time for me to start.

"Five years," I say. "He had done it for five years."

"Something about his daughter being sick," says Andrew, looking to me for my nod. "And the man promised to be crucified every year for five years if she lived."

"It was his last year," I say and always give another quick nod. I don't know if it is true, the part about it being his last year, but it is what I heard that day and is as close to the truth as I can get. Andrew also remembers it that way, because he nods when I say it.

"How?" they want to know, still not waiting for the story.

"How did they do it?"

They don't offer suggestions of how it might have been done. They don't ask, "Was he tied on? Is that what they did? Was he tied on to the cross with a little seat for him to sit on?"

They don't ask, "Was he doped, tranquilized like in those Arab countries before they behead somebody or cut off their hands?" You might expect that, for them to search for a softness in the story, something to make it easier for them, but they don't.

"How did they do it?" is what they want to know. Three nails and a hammer. That's how you do it every time. Of course, first you make the poor bastard carry the cross up and mountain and beat him along the way. That's what you could say to them but you don't.

"Nails," I tell them and jab one finger into my palm. "With nails in the hands. They nailed him on, like the crucifixion."

And, as it was in the beginning, so it will always be.

"Or maybe here," I say, moving my finger to the wrist. "There was a doctor there to show them where to put the nail so he wouldn't die of shock. You see, he wasn't supposed to die. It was his last year."

*

They always want to know why no one stopped it.

"Where were the police?" one of Andrew's women had cried, her eyes moving quickly from his face to mine. "Why didn't someone stop him?" she cried.

Andrew and I both smile at that or maybe laugh softly. How could anyone, any American, understand?

"Were there priests there? Why didn't they do something?" the one who must have been Catholic wanted to know.

"Because they were part of it," I say. "It was like a party, a holiday."

"There were thousands of people there," Andrew says and looks at me.

"One hundred thousand," I say.

"That many? I can't believe there were that many." He says it every time.

"That's what they said in the paper the next year when they also said no one was ever really crucified," I tell him and we laugh together, looking at each other as though no one else is in the room.

"They came from all over Mexico to see it," Andrew tells the listener.

"The fields were covered with people and they were all dressed in those white pajamas. Peasants, real peasants," I tell them.

They are always leaning forward now, glasses clinched in their hands. Andrew's and my glasses are usually moving, from hand to mouth to table, slowly, steadily. Perhaps he will ask me at this point, "Need another?" but I believe that when the story is going well, he does not ask. We continue, moving through the silence to the telling.

"A real fiesta," Andrew says. "People were selling Coca-Cola, food, souvenirs."

I don't remember souvenirs but I remember the people selling their sticky candy from trays hung around their necks, that yellow, flat candy made out of some kind of jelly. I remember the ones pushing the dripping wet bottles of soda at us as we walked up that road with hundreds of others. It was hot and dusty and the road was nothing but a dirt path leading from the town outside Mexico City to the crucifixion.

Twelve of us were there that day. Becky and Joe had come and Ricardo who was half French and half Mexican and in love with my roommate

Cynthia, although I could never understand why. She was there with her long, thin, black hair parted in the middle so both sides fell across her face leaving only this pointed little nose and chin poking out.

Michael O'Brien, the big Irishman from Minnesota, had come. He had just flunked out of college up there but he didn't care. He still wasn't big enough to play football for them. He had come down to visit friends at the American university. Later he joined the Army and went to Viet Nam. I never heard anything else about him.

Shotzy, the tough little redheaded stewardess from Detroit was with us. It was Shotzy who told me about the crucifixion. She had been there the year before but had left early and saw almost nothing. So I really didn't know what was going to happen.

Marjorie, good old Marjorie, was with Andrew. They left Mexico together a few months after the crucifixion and moved to Chicago. Terry was there too, all two hundred and eighty pounds of him, dressed as always like the Mr. Big character in a Humphrey Bogart movie, white wrinkled suit and a Panama hat. Tagging along and sniffing after Shotzy was Tim, little and ugly with kinky brown hair and freckles. He was down on spring vacation visiting his dad at the embassy and latching on to us wherever we went.

And then there was Paul, handsome, tall, mean Paul. My own true love. He had been complaining from the minute we left the city. That was the way he was, always complaining about me and how I made his life so miserable.

But all Andrew or I say is that there were ten or twelve of us that day. We don't count them out and we don't talk much about our walk up the road, nor do I when I tell the story alone. We say nothing other than that it was hot and they were selling things and it took us an hour to reach the mountain.

The mountain was more a craggy hill and I had told them this must be the place where it would happen. Even at a distance it looked too steep but I kept thinking there would have to be a way for the cross to be planted on top. I thought maybe there was another road we couldn't see that wrapped around the back of the mountain, that they would bring the cross up that way. They certainly couldn't bring it up the same road we walked because at the end we had to climb hand over hand, holding onto bushes and rocks to pull ourselves up, to get a seat above the place they would hang him so we could look down on it all.

I tell the listeners how we perched ourselves on the side of the mountain and watched below for a sign that the crucifixion would be there, somewhere. I tell them only four of us made it up there, my boyfriend Paul and I and Ricardo and his girlfriend Cynthia. Andrew didn't make it up that high, I tell them, and he nods with my words. I tell them the others, like Becky and Joe, fell away long before we reached the hill. Terry told us later how he never went further than a seat under a shady tree near the road. There he sat for hours waiting for our return. He saw nothing of what happened.

He only saw the candy sellers and all those others who kept moving up and down the road.

"Then," I pause for a second, "they start to stone us."

"You're kidding," says Andrew. He never remembers this part. I go on.

"There were these people sitting above us on this little mountain and all of a sudden I felt something hit me, like a sting or something." I wince and jerk my shoulder to show them how it was, the first hit.

"I look behind me and all these guys are sitting there, just smiling, like nothing is going on.

"Then these rocks start falling, pebbles first and then they got bigger and bigger and bigger, bouncing all around us." My words are coming faster now, like the rocks.

I don't tell them how Ricardo warned me when I turned to look at those behind us. "Don't look at them, Gloria," he said. "Look down." It was because of my eyes, I thought. He didn't want them to see my light eyes. But, I did look at them. I peeked up at them and they were all staring at me, sitting, crouched like animals and I could see they had moved closer.

I tell them, "In front of me there is this little boy and all of a sudden something hits him and his head opens up like a melon." I open my hands from the prayer position to show them how his head split as though halved, each half falling into a palm.

"I don't remember that at all," Andrew says, his voice hoarse.

"You weren't there," I remind him. "You were below us on the hill. You were with Marjorie. Remember Marjorie?" I sing her name and roll my eyes.

"What happened to him?" the women demand, bringing me back. "What happened to the little boy?"

But I have passed that. I shrug. "Oh, someone helped him. The Red Cross was there or the Green Cross. Whatever."

I say it the same way I felt that day, that it didn't matter. We didn't know what happened to the boy. We didn't stay to find out. Besides, Andrew gets anxious here to get the story back on its way, to move it along to where he is back in it. So I don't tell them how they chased us down the mountain.

*

The times I have told the story without Andrew, I felt empty and then ashamed, like after sex with a man I didn't care about or one who didn't care much about me. I felt as though I had stripped for them, paraded naked for them, wearing only high heels, looking over my shoulder at them, flirting. After I finished telling the story those times, I ran away and left them sitting there.

The first time it was a Navajo artist, a good one. I was working for an advertising agency in Scottsdale. They needed a press kit on him for a local gallery opening. I went up to Flagstaff to talk to him and see his work. For two hours he told me stories about his childhood, his family, his people and what drove him to his art and what kept him painting. When there was nothing else I needed to hear, I turned off my tape recorder and told him about the crucifixion.

I said, "I saw a man crucified once."

He was shocked silent by the story. He sat there in his rocking chair, his arms wrapped across his chest, holding on to himself. I don't remember him asking me one question. I packed up and went back to Scottsdale. Two or three days later I realized I had a terrible crush on this man, a giddy, schoolgirl crush and I prayed he would call, this married-with-two-children Navajo artist. He didn't. I am not surprised.

Then, the newspaper reporter. I told him after a long, good afternoon of conversation which started with an early lunch and stretched out for hours. It was always like that when we talked. He was one of the few people I knew in Scottsdale who seemed interested in life, excited by it. Perhaps I finally told him the story to show him how exciting I was.

Like the artist, the story shocked him into silence but later he called, three times that night. He said he couldn't get the story out of his mind. He thought I should write it, sell it to a magazine. He could see how it could be done, a story about this American girl who thinks she is going to have a great day being a tourist in Mexico and sees a crucifixion instead.

"I really think you need to write it," he said and he sounded worried, upset.

"It does have an effect, doesn't it?" I said.

"And it would sell," he said. "I know you could sell it." That was the real bottom line for him, that the little story could be sold.

I didn't talk to him much after that. He called a few times but we never had the long, lingering talks we once had. Maybe I had reached the end with him so I told him the story. Maybe the telling was the end or maybe the end came with his line about selling it. It certainly doesn't matter now.

With Andrew, I have never felt bad after the story. We linger, especially him. We stay late at the dinner table with brandy or Grand Marnier and coffee after the audience has gone to bed. We go out to the patio or take a walk down the dark street with those Sedona red-rock mountains looming out there in the darkness. He talks then about his feelings for me, the Mexico feelings.

He had a crush on me in Mexico. He has told me that after each time we've told the story. And he asks me, every time, "Didn't you know?"

I always shake my head and laugh and say no because I didn't know then and I don't know now. I am not sure there ever was a crush. Maybe it is only the feeling he gets after we tell the story. But if he did have the feeling back then, I wish I had known. I think I do. It might have made that time easier.

Paul didn't care about me. I knew that. On that day he hung back, pretending he wasn't with me or with any of us. He hated the crowds and the dirt and the noise. He was angry that I made him come. Still, when we finally ended up on the small grassy field, there were only the three of us left, Andrew and I and Paul. Everyone else had disappeared and we were standing there alone with a hundred thousand people standing in the fields below us.

"Like a blanket," is how I describe it. "We were alone in this field, these little white faces, and below us," here I raise my arms and move them apart in a flowing motion," were these thousands of people."

It was then, in that green field with the black and white blanket below us, that I realized something was terribly wrong. The realization hadn't come with the boy's head opening like a melon but with what I could see moving on the road which ran beneath the rise of one side of our field. What I saw made me know I was wrong about the whole idea of the day. I knew then, at that instant, that what was going to happen would be very, very bad.

I think I said then, "Oh, no, no, I don't want to be here." But I don't tell them that, the listeners, and I doubt Andrew or Paul heard me on that day.

2

I still have a dream about chucking it all and taking the train from Laredo, the way Becky used to, rocking and rolling across the desert in my own compartment, seeing the country and then getting off at Guanajuato or wherever it stops. From there I'd go to San Miguel de Allende and find an apartment. I'd become one of those Americans who lives somewhere else.

I even get to the point of trying to figure out what kind of laptop I would take so I could work on my screenplay. I've actually gone into stores to find the right, skinny little laptop to take on the trip back and then worried about the printer I would need to see the written page.

I can see myself walking through the streets in the morning with everybody knowing me and calling to me: "Señorita." And I would look so pretty with my long red hair and my blue eyes. Everyone would know me. I think that a lot.

Which isn't exactly what happened when I did go back. I was thirty-five when I went back to the country of the crucifixion. First, I went to Mexico City.

The city hadn't changed at all. The Reforma was just as grand and exciting. I ate alone on the rooftop terrace of the Majestic Hotel and took pictures of the Zocalo below. I walked through the

National Palace alone and studied the murals of Rivera. I walked the streets of Polanco near Ricardo's apartment and then, after three days, took a bus to San Miguel.

I had been there once before, a trip I did not organize, and so it was rather dull. We spent a day and a night in a small hotel with a small pool and a fly-filled kitchen. One night with Paul, one night of walking the streets with him in his silence. God, how he hated me. Becky and Joe were with us, walking in front of us, hand in hand, laughing, or rather, she laughing at him laughing. They had a good time. I did not and Paul was filled with his hate. This was after the crucifixion. Paul hated me before the crucifixion so any theory that something changed after that day is not where we are going now.

Now we are going to San Miguel and the streets that rise to the filigree-towered cathedral and the plaza where, the second time I was there, they were making a movie. Fifteen, even ten years before, they would have asked me, flirted with me. The director in his open shirt and gold religious medals lying on his hairless chest would have stopped me and asked me to be in his movie, perhaps in the background, walking through, an American. He would have at least asked me or looked at me. Not this time, not at thirty-five.

The first trip to San Miguel had been in the spring. Joe would marry his pretty Becky within a few months. I didn't know that was going to happen. Becky and I weren't close. We were both American girls who had dated Mexicans a few times and who were now back to Americans. American men, for me, were always tall and predictable.

Andrew once told me that one of his reasons for never saying anything about his crush when we were in Mexico was because I was always with Paul.

"Yes, I said, "but I didn't like him, not really."

"Then why did you stay with him?" he wanted to know.

"Because he was an American and I needed friends," I told him.

I needed people to organize and take on exciting trips to places they didn't want to go. There were too many tequila hangovers, too much to do that didn't have to be done, too many touch football games to play, too many car engines that could be pulled apart, pieces spread over the floor for months, tiny little pieces that big-fisted American boys could fiddle with for hours. That's what they wanted to do, not take my trips. But I needed them, the big Americans, and they, I suppose, tolerated me.

I did give up trying to organize events, happenings, lives, but not until five years ago. Even after the crucifixion, I believed that things could be organized, pushed, created. I believed that if you smiled hard enough, worked hard enough, cared enough, spent enough hours awake and worrying, you could make a difference, change people and the way things turned out. You can't.

*

As it turned out, I didn't take the train to San Miguel that second time. I took a plane and not because Andrew had screamed when I told him I was thinking of the train trip. He had shouted at me about how dangerous it would be and how stupid I was being. No, I took the plane because I didn't want to be alone for days on the train. When you are alone in Mexico you can be scared. Besides, the plane was easier.

I gave up my apartment, put everything I owned in storage. I was going back to Mexico to study, Spanish this time. It had been archeology the first time around. Thirty-five and off again. We Americans are like that. We like these new starts. Or rather, we like creating an ending so we can move on.

We like endings, endings to marriages, careers. We can erase our mistakes. Men divorce their wives at forty-five, marry a twenty-four-year-old and gleefully have a whole new family, rushing to get on television or in a magazine to tell the world how wonderful it is, that they will be able to spend more time with this new family then they did the first one. I always wonder what happened to their earlier mistakes, the beginnings. Thrown away, bad job, do again.

I had hit my own ending. I told people at the gas company where I was doing PR exactly why I was leaving. I really didn't care if natural gas was safe or clean or cheap. I was going to be a teacher, not a flack. I was going to go back to my Spanish, my first love, which it wasn't. I could teach, have my summers off to work on my screenplays, to travel. The perfect life, the perfect job. But, to get there, I needed to study once again, one-on-one, hand-in-hand, cheek-to-cheek. If I went to Mexico, to San Miguel, everything would fall into place, no planning required.

"You can't be serious," one of the vice presidents said.

"Why not?" said someone else. "You only live once."

Twice, if you are an American, or three or four times. You can change your life like underwear, everything new and clean. Only this time, I had rummaged around the laundry basket until I found a pair of panties barely soiled and I put them on again. I was going back to where it all began, refusing to think I would find nothing, that the woman I started to be there, the one I could have been, was gone, dead, Americanized, Martinized, safe and sound with money in a retirement account and silky, almost new underwear.

I did have $4,000 in the bank, enough to stay one year if I was careful, even if the peso was falling like a rock. I didn't plan for a year though. A few months at the Institute in San Miguel brushing up on my Spanish and then we would see.

I stayed with Ricardo in Mexico City, the lover of Cynthia with the pointed face. He had just divorced for the second time and had no real interest in me outside of a few old memories. At dinner my second night in the city, he started talking about Americans.

"God, you know what I hate about Americans? This thing about cigarettes." He was saying this as he smoked one. "I was in New York, smoking in this restaurant and this woman turned and screamed at me. Screamed at me because I was smoking a cigarette. Do you believe it?"

Of course I believed it.

"How dare she? Who does she think she is, screaming at me? I told her to go fuck herself."

I agreed with a nod but he went on and I said nothing. He was talking fast, the wide tooth-gritted smile under the Zapata moustache, the cigarette between his fingers close to his face, the wide dark eyes, the leaning into me to share this story of American insanity. Right then he reminded me of another man in another place.

The drunk I once loved, or thought I loved, he too had leaned and leered at me in the same way when he told me a drug addict we both knew couldn't believe that everyone knew he was a user.

"Can you believe that?" he had shouted. Then too there had been that same feeling of, "Watch out, hysterical laughter comes next," that I was now feeling with Ricardo.

I suppose the drunk was daring me to say, "Well, everyone knows you are a drunk. So?" Instead, I gave a shrug of my shoulders.

Later that night he and I had a horrible, crazy fight where he ended up threatening to hit me and I end up at a meeting of Alcoholics Anonymous trying to figure out if he could actually do what those poor people were doing at that meeting. He couldn't, of course.

That is what I was thinking about as Ricardo went on and on about Americans and cigarettes. I was also thinking I had been in this restaurant before, fifteen years before, although I couldn't remember with whom, a man though, an American.

"God, just living in this town is like smoking two packs a day. What difference does it make?" Ricardo wanted to know. I could have said, "Why add to the problem?" but I didn't and he kept on talking.

"You know what else is wrong with Americans?" I didn't.

"You think everything that happens to you is so damn important. One idiot gets shot by some other idiot in Iran or gets taken hostage in Lebanon and if he is an American the whole goddamn world is supposed to stop. God, that is stupid. Who cares? The whole world is dying, starving, wars all over the place and you lose one or two idiots who weren't supposed to be there in the first place and we are all supposed to care. I can't stand that."

I nodded my agreement and I do agree. I did that night, but I didn't like the one-sided conversation and his anger, his begging me for an argument I didn't have in me. I realized then I didn't like him much, probably never had. After all, he liked Cynthia and I could never understand that.

He died in the earthquake a year later with ten thousand other Mexicans. A few years after that, one man died in the quake in San Francisco and this country went crazy. I thought then how Ricardo would have loved that. I think the same every time this country has a disaster, a hundred people compared to Ricardo's ten thousand. Yeah,

Ricardo would have loved it but he was busy being a doctor when his quake hit and was never seen again.

I think he was taking drugs that second trip down. Still, when I watched the Mexican earthquake on television like it was a nightly show the way Viet Nam had been, I didn't know he was under there, unfound by the sniffing, salivating dogs and the poor Mexicans with their bleeding hands, searching, digging, after the Americans and the French and whoever else said it was too late, took their own dogs and left. It was too late but Ricardo was still under there. I hope he died fast and was drugged-up when he did.

Ricardo hadn't wanted to come with us to the crucifixion. He had stopped by the apartment but said no, shaking his head. Perhaps it was too Mexican for him. Perhaps we were too American. In the end, though, he did come, with Cynthia.

*

I used to have this other dream, that I would be back in Mexico City riding down the Reforma in a cab and I would see someone standing on a corner waiting for the light to change, someone from the old days. Or, I would be walking down the streets in the Zona Rosa and I would see an American, one of those who had lived there my first time. He would grab me and say, "Gloria, I can't believe it. You look great."

Then I go back and who did I see? No one. I walked the streets waiting for the face to call to me in the Zona, on the Reforma, in the lobby of the Maria Isabel. There was no one. So much for dreams. There were, however, two memorable encounters.

After dinner that second night, Ricardo stopped in a shop for another pack of cigarettes while I waited for him outside in the yellow lights of the Calle Niza.

I heard this little voice. "You are alone, señorita?" That was all he said. He was young, younger than I was my first time in Mexico, and he was thin and poorly dressed but I smiled at him. As young as I ever was, he was, so I smiled.

"My friend is in the store," I told him in Spanish. "I'm waiting for him."

Now his voice got louder. "Ah," he said, "I am sorry. I didn't mean to bother you. Excuse me." He was rushing through the words and backing away. I laughed, happy that I was once again, even in that yellow light, young to him. I didn't tell Ricardo about that boy. Why bother?

The compliment of being young again, young enough for that thin boy to notice me, is gone now because I have finally figured out what was going on. It took me all this time and while I still don't completely admit it, I think I have to accept a little truth. The truth came to me, as it often does, with another encounter that made the first one clear.

The next day I was getting into a cab in front of the Museum of Anthropology. Suddenly there was this man right next to me, his hand on the car door.

"Can I use this with you?" he said. "I have to go downtown."

I didn't think it was strange or maybe I did and I ignored it, that he would want to share a cab when every other car in Mexico City is a cab or that this one was pointed away from the city toward Ricardo's apartment. Would he have gone with me to Polanco, if that's where I had insisted on going? Could be.

But I said, "Sure." He looked all right, quite all right. He was in his early thirties, dressed all in beige, beige slacks, shoes and a soft beige sweater. He was carrying a small black leather pouch, the male pocketbook of the '80s. We rode together to the Zona Rosa. I stopped at the money changers and he waited out on the street. Then we went to Sanborn's for lunch.

"You want to go to the pyramids tomorrow?" he asked me after I had told him how much I wanted to do just that.

"I will take you there," he said. "I will call you and then come pick you up."

Why not, I thought, although a few minutes before lunch I had been wondering why a good Mexican doesn't have a car. Where is this man's car? But he told me he lived in Ciudad Satelite and I decided it was easier for him to catch a cab from that part of the city then to drive a car downtown.

"A man might answer," I told him when I gave him Ricardo's phone number and address.

"A man?" he said. He was surprised. I told him Ricardo was a friend, only a friend.

"A maricon?" he asked, using the Spanish word for queer. I don't know if there is a nicer word. In Puerto Rico, I once heard a man called a mariposa, a butterfly, but maybe that is only used there.

No, I told him, Ricardo is not gay but a good friend. No matter. The man in beige never called. He paid for lunch so I knew he was on the up-and-up but he never came to take me to the pyramids. I waited for hours that next day. Finally, I wrote a note to Ricardo thanking him and left it balanced against a vase with a single rose I bought for him from the flower cart near the apartment. Then I went to San Miguel. I never saw Ricardo again.

I did try calling him a few months later but he was not at his old number. There was no point in trying right after the earthquake. I also sent him a card but there was no answer. I didn't think about him for awhile. Then, at a party in Phoenix, some-one who had been in Mexico in the '70s and who had known Ricardo told me he heard he had died in the earthquake. He said he heard they had found Ricardo's body covering the body of the man he had been operating on, like he was protecting him, his patient. They always say something like that, don't they, Americans and Mexicans?

So, why didn't the man in beige come to call? I didn't know then and tried not to care but now I think I know. I was neither young nor tempting, I suppose, day or night. I was thin, almost as thin as the Mexican who asked if I was alone, and I looked rich, I suppose. To the man in beige, I looked like an American woman traveling alone.

Do you think he was a gigolo, that man? Do you think my refusal, my lack of movement to pick up the check and the fact that a man would answer the phone, a man who was neither gay nor having an affair with me, put him off his feed, so to speak? Was it simply too complicated for him? Was I too old or was it because I was too young, too naïve, that I wasn't picking up on the message and the message was that I was an American woman looking for something and he could help me find it? Pshaw. He didn't come to take me to the pyramids and that was that.

As for the boy, he may have been starting his career. He was smoking, I remember that, Raleigh Con Filtro, no doubt. He was so young he couldn't have been at the crucifixion. He couldn't even have been that boy whose head split in half.

3

I don't remember exactly when it was or where I was when Andrew first asked me about the crucifixion. It was a few years after Mexico and I hadn't thought about it once. Andrew and I had kept up with each other with phone calls and I had even visited him and Marjorie in Chicago but we had never talked about the crucifixion.

It was very late the night he called to ask me about it, and he was talking very softly as though he didn't want Marjorie to hear him. He said, "I know this sounds crazy but I have to ask you something."

"Okay," I said. "Go ahead."

"Do you remember the crucifixion?" he asked me. I don't think I said anything for a few seconds.

"Yeah," I must have finally said, "I remember."

"Wow," he said with this kind of sigh. "I kept thinking it was some kind of dream. I had to call you to find out if it really happened but I felt so stupid. I've asked Marjorie about it but she doesn't remember it the way I do. So, it really did happen, Gloria?"

"She wasn't there," I told him. "She didn't see what we saw."

"She didn't?" He had forgotten that, that Marjorie hadn't been with us in the field.

"No, she wasn't where we were. Remember,

Andrew? You and I and Paul ended up alone in that field. I remember it all. It wasn't a dream."

I did remember then, as clearly as if we were standing there in that grassy field. But Andrew was still in his own world, trying to find the memory.

"I even tried to find Joe's number in Dallas," he told me. "I wanted to ask him if he remembers what happened that day, to see if I was remembering it right."

"He wasn't there either," I told him. "Not where we were."

"But it did happen?"

"Oh yeah, it happened," I said.

"I thought so," he said and gave this little sigh and that was the end of our conversation that night.

*

Telling the part about what happened in the field is difficult. For one thing, the setting is hard to describe. You could call it a grassy knoll except there is only one grassy knoll for those of us who remember, the one where someone stood and did or didn't shoot Kennedy. I tell the part about our grassy knoll using my hands, like the Mexicans or Italians do, to show the listeners what it was like.

"It was this grassy field above the road and we were on it all by ourselves, the three of us, Andrew and me and my boyfriend Paul."

I tell them how the road we had walked up to reach the mountain ran along the bottom of our field. When we came back down that road, we still didn't know where the crucifixion would be. There was no way to ask anyone. What could you say? Hey, where's the crucifixion? Where's the celebration?

No, I wanted the day to be serious, not a tourist trip. I was holding on to that, even after the stoning, showing everyone that we weren't there as tourists, that we actually cared about all of this.

The field was right there, a step above the road, so we went to it, walked to the middle of it and stood there looking down at the people in the fields below the road.

"And all of a sudden they would start moving, running from one side of the field to the other," I tell them and move my hands like the soft rolling of a wave. "They kept thinking something was happening so they'd move toward it, all together, and then change and move to the other side."

They were moving toward a road we hadn't seen on our trip up the mountain. This was the road that forked off the main road and ran along one side of our field. Now could we see the fork but this other road disappeared beneath the green rise of the field. I knew this was the way he had to come.

I tell them, "I was looking that way, toward the second road, and then I saw it."

Andrew had just asked me what we were supposed to do now, what was going to happen now, and Paul was scuffling his feet in the dirt and grass, unhappy he had been dragged someplace else he didn't want to go, when I turned slightly to my right. I saw the horsemen, two of them, dressed like Roman soldiers. They were wearing metal breastplates and plumed helmets. When I tell this part I motion over the top of my head, showing the height and length of the plume or brush on their helmets.

Their legs are bare and they hang down along the horses' sides. I can only see as far as their knees because the roll of the field cuts off my view of the road.

I feel it now, the sickness I felt then, the shock of knowing what was happening, what was going to happen. This is the point where I want to get up and walk away from the story, to take a quick drink, to look out to the night, but the words keep coming.

"I see this man on horseback and he is dressed like a Roman with this helmet with a plume," and here I make that motion over the top of my head.

"There was more than one soldier," Andrew will remind me but I don't stop to agree, to change my words.

"And I could see how he was beating on something below him. His arm going up and down, hitting at this thing with a stick or a whip handle. But I can't see what it is he is hitting because the rise of the field cuts off our view of the whole road.

"But he is hitting at the thing, hard." I make the hard, fast motions of the beating with my arm. The words are hard and fast-moving as well.

"The crowd was going crazy," Andrew tells them. "They've all rushed to that side of the fields to see what was going on," I tell them.

"And the noise was unbelievable," Andrew

will say. "Everyone was screaming, everyone. I never heard anything like that in my life," he says, shaking his head.

I don't remember it as screaming, more like a sighing. But I don't know what makes a person sigh like that. Maybe lovemaking or something like the sight of a million-dollar Arab stallion coming into the show ring for the first time. But there would be more joy in that sigh. This sigh was like nothing I have ever heard before or since.

"Oh, God," I must have said then, "Oh, God," because I could see something else. I could see the top of a cross moving, then stopping and then disappearing from view. Without seeing him, I knew there was a man beneath it, bent and stumbling with the weight of the cross on his back. I couldn't see him but I could see that horseman beating him, the hate and the anger, the arm going up and down.

I knew Andrew and Paul were staring with me. They had to be. Where else would you look? I was sick then. I wanted to throw up. Then the top of the cross was back into view, moving slowly, so horribly slowly and the horseman kept beating at the thing below him.

"Jesus," I say softly at this part. "It was awful."

*

Andrew always lets me tell this part about the horseman with the whip and the top of the cross moving beyond the rise and it is the part I tell best,

I think, because I was the one who saw it first and because I was the one who organized the whole thing.

Oh, how I had organized it, that damned tourist trip to the crucifixion. I pushed at all of them to go. I told them how wonderful it would be. I made them leave their cameras home to show our respect. I even made a costume for the party, low heeled shoes, longish skirt, white blouse. I wore a tiny cross my mother had given me for some birthday. There I was, the whitest, rottenest, stupidest American of them all and I had brought my friends. We were stoned, chased and, no doubt, somewhere along the line, spat on.

I was also the Catholic. I was the one raised with the religion that made such a godawful event out of the whole damn thing.

4

I think it's mean, the way Andrew and I do this, almost evil in a way. But, that doesn't stop me. The story is like a play and hasn't changed since the very first time. We both know our lines and our parts and we do it the same every time. The way we do it no one can get up and walk away. Well, maybe they could but I don't know how. Besides, nobody has ever told us to stop or told us they didn't want to hear anymore. They always let us go through to the end.

We start with the first drink and when we're finished, it's time for dinner. We don't talk about it after that. Neither do they, but it leaves a strange feeling around the dinner and the night. I know that.

The first time we told it the visitor was a girl he had brought from San Francisco. I had driven up from Scottsdale for the weekend. After we finished the story that night, I could hear his mother talking to him in the kitchen.

"You never told me that story, Andrew. Why didn't you tell me about that?" she said. She sounded hurt and sad that he had seen something like that and had never told her. The girl, on the other hand, didn't say much of anything.

The second woman was in banking, marketing I think.

She listened to the story and went to bed right after dinner.

Then there was the computer date from Long Beach or someplace. She didn't like the story and she didn't like me. She was in corporate communications. I didn't bother telling her about the advertising and PR work I did. She stuck to us like glue when we went out to the patio for our after-dinner talk. She even began our walk with us, so puffed up with how much she didn't like me or the night that she walked with her arms held tight across her chest. Finally, she announced that she was going back, she was too cold and too tired to keep on. We let her go back to the house alone. She was out of his life by the next time he called to talk.

The last time I was there, Andrew was without a woman and his parents had guests for dinner. They were a young couple who had just started collecting Western art. They had bought one of his father's paintings and had been invited to stay for dinner. We didn't tell the story that night and there was no after-dinner walk or talk of Andrew's Mexico crush. That was a couple of years ago and I haven't seen him since.

We do exchange Christmas cards and he checks in every once in a while. The last time was about six months ago. He called and told me he was seeing someone special.

"We have so much in common," he told me. "We agree on everything."

That's the same thing he said when he called about meeting the computer date.

"She's just like me," he said and before I could

say it, he started to laugh and said, "Well, yes, I suppose she would be, a computer date and all."

Right, Andrew.

Now he's saying about the new one, "You wouldn't believe how much alike we are."

No, probably not, but if he marries this one I don't think I will hear from him for a long, long time, if ever.

*

The talk about his crush is all part of the ritual, another little story. We always say the same things. It's gentle, an ending to the night, like the conversation you have after making love, that talking over the cigarettes we all so enjoyed smoking before we were told to stop.

I remember how it was at twenty, the lighting of that cigarette after sex with Paul. I do remember that cigarette and the sound of fumbling and then the match being struck and the sigh as he leaned back against the headboard. Or, maybe it was me with the sheet pulled above my breasts, tight, leaning over to the nightstand, fumbling for that cigarette and then lying back with a coy smile of how nice it all was when it wasn't nice at all. Was that only after the crucifixion? No, sex with Paul was always that way.

Sex was not bad with Paul, not good, not bad. He thought his penis was too small. Perhaps it was. His was smaller than others I have known, almost the smallest. There was a man I knew with a penis that rose above his belly like a tiny tree, a bonsai tree. He was a big man. That made the size so surprising. I didn't make love with him. I didn't want to even before the penis. Did he know how small it was? I wonder.

One night after a heavy duty party in Mexico, Joe asked me why I bothered with Paul at all. He said, "Why do you waste your time with him?" He said he liked Paul but he didn't like the way he treated me.

"Why do you stay with him?" he wanted to know. Because he was my choice for that year and I wasn't thinking much that year.

I know he is a tired old man by now, living in that small town in Tennessee, probably bald. I know his equipment didn't grow. It wouldn't have helped anyway unless he wore it on the outside of his pants.

The first time I was in San Miguel, I never saw the cathedral, the plaza, anyone making movies. I saw nothing but that pool we sat by and the cobblestone streets we walked. That is because my eyes were always down as Paul, tall and good looking, suffered in his awful silence with the thought that I should have brought him to this place. Joe and Becky spent all their time laughing. Joe never had to wear his on the outside of his pants.

5

Well, would I change my life, meet the man, get a job, after my year in San Miguel? No, and it wasn't going to be a year or even six months. But anyone who says you can't go back again is wrong. San Miguel the second time was wonderful.

San Miguel is a good town for leftover hippies who joined the establishment but figured out how to have jobs that let them stay in the '60s. I saw them at the small hotel where I stayed and at the Institute where I took Spanish. They had their blue book bags or blue baby carriers on their backs and Birkenstocks on their feet. They were married now, their hair short enough for the colleges that gave them their Mexican sabbaticals and their concerned law firms that handled environmental issues for the good guys and let their attorneys go off every so often for a learning experience. I stayed away from them. I wanted to be part of Mexico again.

At the hotel the maid tells me that the two children I see playing in the kitchen have no home. She tells me the "pobrecitos" need a mother. She also tells me it is "que lastima," what a shame, that I have never married.

They are pretty little children, a girl and a boy. They have that soft brown skin, thick black hair, those big sad eyes like the old Keane paintings in the '60s.

"They have no life here," the maid tells me. "You have so much in the United States, not like Mexico."

Two homeless children and I am thirty-five. They could be mine, I think. Why not? Other people have done it. I mention them, the little boy and the little girl, on my weekly call to my dad. I wonder out loud what I could do to help them.

"I don't know what you could do for them," my dad says. "Nothing, probably."

"I might like to take care of them," I say to him, hoping he'll agree to the possibility. "I'm good with kids."

"You never liked being around children," he tells me. "You would have had your own by now if you did. Your sister Jeanne was the one who always liked children, even when she was little. I don't think you ever played with dolls. Did you?"

No, but I could like children. I liked these kids. I spent every afternoon with them. I bought them food, took them for walks through the market. I played with them in the hotel garden. The fat cook was their cousin or a cousin of their mother, the maid told me. She took care of them. She would also smile all over me saying what a good señorita I was, what a pretty señorita, how the children loved me, and what a poor señorita I was without children, without family.

Oh, God, here it is. I can change my life in an instant, change it completely. The thought hit me like lightening bolt. This was my future. I could take them back to the U.S., my new children. I could settle down somewhere, work my eight hours a day for my new family. I will move to Idaho, live near the mountains, build a log cabin from a kit, raise my children, my Maria and Carlos.

What will they call me instead of señorita? Tia Gloria? Perhaps, but then I think it sounds too much like an after-dinner drink. We will need something else. All I know now is that the change is possible. I only have to take the first step

I could call Jeanne and tell her what I am thinking about doing. After all, she is the mother in the family. She is the one with two step-children, the house in Arlington, the two silver Volvos, the husband with the job in the government. This is her second husband. When the first one found out Jeanne couldn't have children, he refused to consider an adoption, of a boy, anyway.

"I don't want some other man's baby," he used to say. "Maybe a girl, but I don't want a boy who isn't mine to have my name." What a charmer. He went on to a younger wife who could have babies and has produced two girls so far. Good.

But, I don't call Jeanne, not about my children. Instead I start talking to the Americans, the ex-hippies and bright smiling yuppies. I tell them how the more I know these children, the more I am considering the possibility of talking to someone about taking care of them. My concern, I tell them, is whether or not I could do it, take care of two children.

Sure, they tell me. Well, look at them. They have a split working day, husband and wife each doing the same job but at different hours, or they have the best nanny on earth, or they are hand painting postcards for their Carmel bookstore and coffee shop. Sure, it can be done. Hypothetically, of course.

Now I am talking about nothing else and thinking about nothing else. We could have a dog, a goat, a horse. I'm not that old, not for older children. They are six and eight so it is more like I am a new mother at twenty-eight. That makes sense.

The more I talk about this to the Americans, to myself, the faster I talk, the more ifs and what-ifs I start to bring up. I am saying things to the Americans like, "Commitment always brings a kind of panic, doesn't it? I mean it's natural, isn't it, to worry about this kind of decision?"

I see the children for hours every day and I am telling myself I am going to have to make a decision. Do I want them? Do I want them forever? Why can't I decide? What is in me that prevents me from making a normal decision? Why do I fight it?

"I really like these kids," I tell my dad. "They don't have anybody and they are good kids. You'd like them," I say, trying to make him respond, to make him say, "Hey, if you want them, go for it."

"Yeah, all children are cute at that age," is what he says. "You were a doll when you were little, so friendly and happy."

What happened?

Now I am lying in bed every night sick with the thought of making this decision, Every day I am saying to the Americans, "It's normal, right, to feel this nervous?" They nod and smile at my constant babbling about these kids. I must have seemed half nuts to them. I was acting as though this was a life-and-death decision that had to be made in a matter of days, not months. I was organizing again, planning a party I really didn't want to give.

Do a lot of unmarried women in their thirties do this, think about adopting a third world child? I think they do. I've read the articles about it, about how they send away to India or Bolivia for some baby. And they always write about how this baby or child has fulfilled their lives. Yet, I couldn't do it even when the kids were right there in front of me. I couldn't say what it was I wanted to do and I couldn't get away from those children.

They waited for me in the mornings, sat in the kitchen waiting for me to come down for my coffee. They waited for me outside the hotel, watching for me to come down the street after classes. They knocked on my door after I came back from an evening out.

I began to avoid them. I stayed out of the kitchen, took my coffee at a cafe near the Institute. I tried to stay away from my room until late at night so I wouldn't hear those sad little knocks. And every day the maid is saying "pobrecitos," and shaking her head.

Half of me was thinking, If I don't do this, my last chance, I will never do anything with my life, never be like everyone else. The other half was dodging the children, the maid. When I was with the children, I was frightened of the way they looked at me, those big sad eyes. At night I was sweating and in a panic, thinking, Here I am in Mexico, scared and sick about something over which nobody has asked for a decision.

I had done this kind of thing once before, gotten crazy with fear over a decision I didn't have to make. It was the same kind of thing, a life change. I was in Tucson doing the research for a brochure and catalog the agency was putting together for a girl's school run by nuns. The school was on the grounds of the convent and I was there for four days working with a local photographer.

I was with those women every waking minute. They told me about how they had come to join the order, how God had chosen them at the lowest moment of their lives, how nothing had worked for them until He, with a capital H, had taken them by the hand. And here we were, in this beautiful, quiet setting, the desert all around us and not a care in the world.

Oh, God, I wanted to be a nun. I was chosen to be a nun. The beauty of the realization flowed over me, the golden light of God descended on me. I had no choice. I was chosen. It was all over but the shouting. Not quite.

It scared the shit out of me. I wanted to get away from that God but, as one of the old nuns said, grabbing onto my arm with those bony skinless fingers, "When God wants you, he gets you."

Alone in the convent, the photographer gone home, with nobody to talk to except the nuns, I locked my door and freaked. Oh, God, did I have to stay here forever with these women. Is that why my relationships with men were so screwed up? Would my only relationship with a man from now on be with the priest all the nuns fretted and giggled over?

That night I was terrified. I vomited I was so frightened. I got down on my knees and said, "God, give me five more years before I have to do this. Let me have another man."

When the photographer came the next morning, I said, "That's it, no more pictures. We're out of here." I had no desire to face my fear. No, thank you.

I told my dad what had happened, how scared I was that one night and he asked me, "What? Did you think they were trying to recruit you?" I didn't say anything.

"Well, they probably were," he said. "They are a cult, you know, as much as any other religious cult. Only, we accept them because they've been around so long. You did the right thing," he told me. "You got out of there. Why are you still so upset about it?"

Because I thought I was running from the inevitable. I didn't run in San Miguel. Not really. I went to a lawyer.

"Hay problemas," was the first thing he said when I asked him, hypothetically, of course, about the possibility of an American woman taking two Mexican orphans back to the U.S.

"Necesitamos papeles especiales, special papers," he said and warned me that you would also need much time, mucho tiempo. Much time and bribes, he meant. He also wasn't sure the government would be happy about an American taking two children out of Mexico. Still, he said it was possible.

He was an older man, hair greying but good-looking. He was wearing a grey suit and the whitest shirt I have ever seen.

"It is you?" he asked.

I may have shrugged but I didn't say it was me.

"Are you married?" he asked me and motioned to the ring on his own finger.

"No."

"That might be a problem," he said.

"Not in the United States," I told him.

"No," he said, "but in Mexico, yes."

I couldn't resist saying, "Of course a person could just take the children and walk across the border like everyone else does."

Now he is shrugging. He knew I wouldn't be back but still he asked in English, "What would you like me to do for you, señorita?"

"Nada, nothing, I only had questions," I told him. "It is something one needs to think about." I stood to leave.

"There is one thing," he said. "Are you sure there is no family, no one at all for the children? That would be muy raro here in Mexico. That is important."

Yes, if I were coming back, but I wasn't. I smiled, shook his hand and left.

Ah, I felt wonderful. I could breathe again. The decision had been made. There were too many complications, special papers, time, and there was the cousin, of course. I didn't need to feel responsible for those children. There was a blood relation. What a relief.

On my way back to the hotel I stopped by the

Institute to take down the phone number from a For Rent notice I had seen earlier. I also stopped to buy presents for Carlos and Maria. He got the fire truck and she got the doll. The next day I left the hotel.

"They will be fine," I assured the cook-cousin.

"Claro," she said. "Of course."

"It is hard to be without parents," I said. "Hard for the children."

"They aren't without parents," she told me. "Without a mother, yes, but their father, my cousin, is in the north, in the United States. He has a good job in a restaurant and sends the money." She said all this while working at the sink and never looking at me. I was shocked. I made her say it again.

"They have a father?"

"A good father, yes, in California. He works hard for his children. Of course, they have a family, like all of us."

The next two months were quiet. I rented a room in Harold and Claude's house. They were gay and had been together for years. When they moved to Mexico, Harold had turned all of their money into pesos and now the bottom was falling out of the exchange rate, dropping a hundred pesos a day, sometimes changing in a matter of hours. Harold was going crazy watching the fall but Claude didn't worry.

Claude started drinking every morning at eleven o'clock, right before the tiny, muscular, senior citizen, American woman showed up to lead him in an aerobic class of one on the patio. Claude would stretch his arms, lift his legs, while holding a drink in one hand and a cigarette in the other.

"Do you believe me?" he would giggle happily. "I'm dying, dying."

I adored both of them.

Every morning I would go to the market with Harold to buy the vegetables and salad greens for the afternoon meal. All the merchants knew him and called to him as he passed or they smiled at him and waved. Claude came with us a few times. I could see the merchants rolling their eyes at his feminine walk, his limp waves. A few may have laughed at him. But Claude would only smile back and happily nod. He knew, I knew, the Mexicans were not being cruel. They are usually very kind to crazy Americans.

In the early evening, the three of us would sit in the living room stuffed with furniture and paintings and wooden carvings of saints with long heads and little bodies, and Harold would talk about what he should sell and when.

"We will be destitute in a couple of months if this keeps up," he would moan.

"Oh, we will not," Claude would flick a hand at him. They would bicker back and forth, Harold saying it was, after all, his mother's money. Claude would say, "Well, I had some too and you put it all in pesos. You said we should."

Together they would study the papers mailed from the bank, trying to figure out what the columns of numbers meant until Claude would get bored and push them away.

"I can't understand any of it," he would say.

I would drink my rum and coke and rest on

the fat couch. So, we would end the day.

At one point Harold asked me if I would mind sharing the house with another American student, a young woman with a little girl. Of course not, I told them, it was their house.

She was gone in two days. She left screaming about how she wasn't going to expose her child, a quiet mousey thing, to AIDS and she couldn't even have a cup of coffee in the morning because of how afraid she was of the disease these men must have.

"I don't care about myself," she said when she was pushing clothes into her canvas carryall. "But, I do care about my child and what she is being exposed to. Don't you read the news? I can't even drink a cup of coffee in this house. I can't used the kitchen."

"Isn't this sort of silly." I said. "All the water is either bottled or boiled before you do anything with it."

"Well, you can stay here if you want to, that's your business, but not me."

There she was, a free spirit from Taos, hair on her legs and under her arms, a child of nature, a liberal to the core and out of that house in less than an hour.

Harold didn't say anything. He seemed more confused than angry. Claude was hurt and he was mad.

"What does she think," he wanted to know, "that we're going to give her big sloppy kisses on the lips? Is that what she's afraid of?"

I didn't know.

I spent the two months with them and then

went back to Arizona. I still have their address and phone number but I never called them. I suppose I was afraid that the pesos would have finally dissolved and the santos and the paintings would have been sold and that one of them would have died by now. I don't know which would be worse, sweet, giggling, aerobics-in-the-morning Claude dying or Harold dying and leaving Claude behind. He wouldn't make it alone.

There was a man on the bus back to Mexico City I have never forgotten. He was in a dark suit, nervous, balding, pale-faced and sweating. He was an American and could not speak a word of Spanish. He was worried about where his ticket would take him and how he would get from there to the airport to catch his flight home. He held a helmet on his lap, the kind welders use with the metal visor that pulls down over the eyes like a knight in the Middle Ages.

"My wife is an artist," he told me as the bus began to move. "A sculptor."

"Ah, yes," I nod to the helmet.

"She lives here, in San Miguel," he said.

Oh, he is going back to the U.S. with her helmet while she stays in San Miguel doing her art. Strange, I thought. He rode the whole way with his hands on the helmet.

Behind me on that bus were two American women talking about the face lift one of them had and the face lift the other was going to have in L.A. They knew each other's doctors by reputation. I waited until the first stop to look at them over the top of the seat, to see which one had the lift. I couldn't tell.

I thought, Is this what I would become if I stayed in places like San Miguel, the single older woman moving from town to town, from lift to lift? I thought then, on that bus, that it was something worth running from.

At one stop there was a beggar with legs like useless bundles of rags. They flung about as he hopped on his butt across the cement to meet each bus as it came in. He had this look of intensity, a look of a man at work, a salesman looking for a sale. I left the bus to buy a soda and when I came back I gave him a pile of pesos, at least five dollars in our money. I waited for the shock to cross his face.

He shoved the pesos in his pocket without looking at me, without a word, and scuttled over to the next bus. Watching him from my seat behind the bus window, I felt like a fool. I wanted him to be overjoyed with my money.

I looked at only one other beggar while I was in Mexico this second time. She was an Indian, young, on the Calle Hamburgo that night with Ricardo. It was after midnight and we were walking back to the Reforma to find a cab. She was putting her family to bed in the doorway of a shop. She was tucking the blanket around her two children, patting at them the way mothers do, worrying over them. I stopped and touched her shoulder. I handed her all the change I had. It wasn't much.

Giving her the money didn't make me feel better or worse. I just thought it would be nice for her to have something to begin the next day. In the past few years, I think that is all I have really wanted, something to begin the next day. I suppose the feeling had already started on that last trip to Mexico.

6

At this part of the story, after we have seen the horsemen, there is a moment of silence. There was the same sort of break that day too when the cross and the horsemen disappeared behind the rise.

Then Andrew said something like, "I don't believe it. Did you see that? Jesus, this is the real thing."

"It was the real thing," he says now. "It must have been exactly like that day when it did happen, the people, the crowds."

Ah yes, but that first time there had been women keening in the corners. That's what the Irish call it, keening, crouching in doorways with shawls over their heads, crying about what is happening. There was no keening this day, no sorrow.

Our audience can't stop listening. They can hardly breathe. Nor can I. That is how it was then, the breaths catching in my throat as I kept adding more and more air.

I look down now at the crowd but I don't see anything, only a white field. I don't think about Paul and Andrew on either side of me. Only I am there and those below me, people without faces. It was like being in a tunnel. It was like being totally alone.

Then I tell the listeners how I see that the whole crowd below is looking up. "Above us, not at us, but over our heads."

I raise my hand and flutter it back over my head. My mouth is tight as though the muscles in my cheeks are pulling it flat. I don't talk to the listeners. I talk above them, the way the crowd looked at us that day, above us.

That's when I turned, when I realized they weren't looking at us. I turned my head slowly, very slowly, to follow their gaze, afraid but knowing what I would see.

"So I turn and start to look over my shoulder because I know that something must be going on behind me." As I say this, I turn slowly in my chair or seat, looking over my shoulder the way I did that day. Then I turn back to the listeners but I didn't turn back to the crowd that day, not then.

"And I see them, as close as that door." I motion to the front door a few yards from where we sit. "Or maybe it was farther, the front lawn. But right above us is this flat part, a little mesa, and I can see the two crosses of the thieves. I can see the two thieves hanging on the crosses at the far end of the mesa."

I don't know if Andrew and Paul turned then, as I did, to stare at the place above us. But I didn't turn my whole body, only my head and my eyes. I did not want to turn my back on those below us. It wasn't fear but I knew I shouldn't turn away from them completely.

"Then I see something else," I tell them.

I breathe hard, even as I tell this now, the panting, the searching for the right words because there may have been something else that made me turn, something besides the crowd's gaze upward. I don't know when it started, before or after I looked over my shoulder, but I heard the sound of hammering and I knew what was being done. They were hammering that man's hands onto the cross.

I hear that sound and I hear the sound of the crowd change, louder now, like a low rumble, more than that, like a sexual sound of pleasure which is hurtful but not evil, that awe of pleasure without rules and truly, completely and always selfish.

Why could I hear the sounds of the hammer so clearly? Simple. With dumb luck, we three white-eyed gringos were standing alone in a field only a few yards below the crucifixion. For all I know, we were on some sort of sacred ground. Maybe that is why nobody else was there with us. Or maybe it was because the three of us formed a kind of barrier to the crowd below.

They all looked above us, to the crosses on the hill, the two men hanging, but we could hear the sounds, or I could hear the sounds of the hammer. My brain is saying, "This isn't happening. This isn't happening. This isn't real. They aren't doing this." But I know it's all true and I still don't turn my body fully away from the crowd.

I wonder if there is ever a time when a hyena faces one threat but still turns to look over his shoulder to see something far worse or something so awful that it stuns him. Does the animal know what is far worse than the danger he understands? I don't know, not about him anyway.

*

I wanted to be an archeologist. That was the reason I was in Mexico. I wanted to discover the tombs in Egypt, to be the first one to see all those things inside them. I wanted to see that mummy man and to know I found him, brought him back to life, that he is living again, contributing again, part of it all again. I wanted to know who he was and how he died and who cried for him when he did. Like the man they found in the Austrian mountains, I wanted to make a connection with the past, to touch the past. That's what I wanted to do.

I knew how to spell archeology when I was two. No big deal. I could also spell encyclopedia. Like everything else, if you can give it a beat, a rhythm, you can remember it.

What did happen was I found out you had to take all those anthropology courses in college and study a few million years or so of men covered with hair, with big foreheads and loose lips, who did absolutely nothing extraordinary but kill animals and, one has to assume, each other. Millions of years of that. I didn't care about that. I wanted to find a tomb, which wasn't hard to do in Mexico. I know the mountain we first sat on for the crucifixion was one of those Aztec temples. Andrew may have even said so at the time.

I am almost certain about that mountain. All of Mexico has these fake mountains. Pyramids, all of them. There isn't enough money or time to dig them out of the earth. There may never be but I would like to do that, I would have. That's why I went to Mexico the first time, to study archeology and to go on a real dig. I was supposed to go on that dig in the summer after a year of classes at the American university but I left in June.

After Mexico I worked in a travel agency, waited tables, drove a trolley for the tourists. I have also cleaned houses, taken care of animals, including ferrets which smelled to high heaven. I didn't have a clue about what I wanted to do. I worked for the money.

The mother of one of my boyfriends told me that since I liked to read, I should work in a bookstore. She was that kind of person, a small thinker. She was also Paul's mother. As unhappy as we were, or he was, we stayed together after Mexico, for a while. All of the couples we knew did.

Paul and I went to Tennessee. His mother lived in a small town a few hours outside of Memphis. She ran the insurance agency her husband had turned over to her as part of the divorce settlement. Paul went back there to hide until he could find out what the U.S. Army and the local draft board had in store for him. He thought he would be okay if he acted like his mother's major support, the George Hamilton thing. I got a job at a travel agency in Memphis and spent my days off visiting Paul and the small town.The setting was pretty, rolling hills, farms, that's how I remember it. The sheriff's wife slept with other men and the sheriff drove a Nova. Nothing else was going on. My goal was clear, to get Paul out of there and away from his mother.

Paul was not a bad man, only weak. His mother, Miz M., as everyone was supposed to call her, was the mother from hell. She was the kind of woman who would serve us dinner, humming around us, fretting, finding the perfect slice of meat or the perfect potato for her Paul, her only child, except for an older daughter who stayed happily away in her own home in Ohio.

She would serve her Paul, her son, and she'd serve me, the girl he brought home from Mexico. She wouldn't sit down during all of this, not for any length of time. She would keep hopping up and getting something else for us, whether we wanted it or not. I would get more and more nervous with all the jumping up and running around and the dishes being pushed at me.

I'd whisper to Paul, "Please tell her to sit down and eat with us."

She would whine in this little girl voice about how she wasn't hungry and then she'd beg for just a little tiny piece of meat, not too much. She actually said, more than once, "Please, just give me the bone. That's all I want."

Paul would give it to her, the steak bone, the piece we would have saved for our dog at home. "That's what she wants," he'd say and laugh if I tugged at him or made a face.

She was also sick a great deal, complaining how she could do it all but she was just a little weak today, but things would be fine now that Paul was there to help her with the business. I thought she was as strong as a horse.

The only answer, as every American woman knows, was to get him out of there, to pry him loose, to promise him that everything would be perfect if we moved away, without any hint that she, the mother, was the root of all his problems, his lack of ambition, the hole in his goals. You didn't tell him that you knew he would be a strong and happy man once you got him away from her.

"We need to go to California," I told him. "We need to get someplace where it's sunny and warm, where we can get a new start."

In Tennessee it was raining and grey and I, born and bred in the Arizona sun, hated it, along with fact that everyone I met there seemed none too bright. Or, if they were smart, they played the dumb hick farmer.

I told Paul we could get a place near the beach and find jobs. It would be better for him than sitting in his mother's insurance agency learning the business. Paul had actually pulled off a degree in business from the school in Mexico. I told him he should use it, that it meant good money in a different place and I certainly needed to do something better with my time than writing tickets for other people's trips out of Memphis.

I harped on it for months until he agreed to leave. I organized the whole thing, of course, where we were going, what we would drive. The car would be a '67 hunter green Mustang convertible I found in Memphis. We were going to California with the top down and our hair blowing in the wind.

I did make it to California. God, how I loved Hermosa Beach. I found a studio apartment a few blocks from the ocean and I got a waitress job in a restaurant on the beach. Paul and the Mustang never made it that far. When we got to Phoenix, he called his mother and then turned around and went back to Tennessee.

She told him she was sick, surprise, surprise, and she needed his help in the business and she would never ever think of asking him to come back if she didn't need him so badly and maybe he could do this whole thing later, this California trip. She must have also told him exactly what she was going to pay him once he got back because his parting line to me was, "My mother can support me much better than I can support myself."

He left and that was that. A few months later I bought a bright red Fiat Spider convertible and drove it to California. The car ran about four days out of seven but it was a great car for the beach. If Paul kept the Mustang, he has a classic now.

That's what men do, isn't it, remember their lives by the cars they drove? They also remember their first loves. That's the high point of their entire love life. Of their whole life, the highest point is war. I know that. They always love a good war because then they are really alive. The fact that they are busy killing everyone else doesn't seem to bother them. They like it. They like the raping. They like the being with men, scratching their butts, their gonads. They like smelling bad. I know that and so do they.

But, get this, nobody I ever went out with, none of my male friends, which includes all the guys from Mexico, ever went anywhere near Viet Nam or the army. Of course, they didn't have to. They were white and going to college. Nobody wanted them, not for killing anyway.

I've had fights with both Andrew and Joe about Viet Nam. They both yell, Joe yells anyway, about how necessary it was, how we could have won if we had done it right. If the hippies let us do it right, says Joe. Boy, how I've wanted to say, especially to Joe, "Well, isn't it too bad you couldn't have gone to Viet Nam to help us win the war." Maybe someday I will.

I never did have any final say with Paul. I did get a final letter though. He had called and asked me for the pink slip on the car. I refused. I said even if he had given me the money for the car, we were both in this thing together. I had more than paid my own way. If he wanted the title, he would have to send me a check for half the value of the car.

He sent a check on his mother's account and a letter full of hate and anger. He wrote I had ruined two years of his life, which it hadn't been, and had cut him off from his friends and his family, such as they were. I had, according to him, almost destroyed him. I threw the letter away and sent the title only after the check cleared the bank.

I had decided he was having some sort of nervous breakdown by the time we got to Phoenix, like Glen Campbell used to say, and it sounded like he finished having it back with mama in Tennessee.

"She always said you'd screw me," is what he wrote in the letter. Yup.

Poor Paul, not only was he dragged another place he didn't want to be but I made him pay for it. I'll give him this, he didn't let me drag him as far as California. He dug in his heels the minute we got to Phoenix, the minute we turned off the freeway.

I had pulled off to get a soda and some change for the phone. I wanted to call Dad to let him know we were in town and on our way to the house. He was at his office and I told his nurse, "Tell him we're here and we're heading in."

While I was doing this, Paul was in the car, sulking as always and watching the people pulling up to the store in their old beat-up trucks. They were the usual raggedy people who hang around convenience stores in Arizona and this wasn't the best part of town.

When I got back into the car, he said to me, "Jesus, Gloria, what kind of town is this? Look at these people. A bunch of drunks and niggers and Mexicans. What kind of place have you brought me to?"

He was out of there in two days. In a few months I had the Fiat and was on my way to California. Dad was living in a townhouse on the side of a golf course in Phoenix. Becky and Joe were happily married and having babies in Dallas. Marjorie and Andrew were living together in Chicago. Ah, American the beautiful.

It was one year after the crucifixion.

7

I grew up in Phoenix, which was once a nice place. We had a house on the edge of the desert, a low, long, ranch house with a shingled roof and a long porch in front which Mom lined with big clay pots full of geraniums. There was a barn in back where Jeanne and I kept our horses. You could still ride your horse down Central Avenue then without worrying about being hit by a car or shot by some gang riding in one.

Dad is a retired doctor, born and raised in Texas. He met my mother while he was in residence in Pennsylvania and together they moved to Arizona. She died of cervical cancer when I was fifteen.

Jeanne is three years older than me and we both made it through the death okay. She left after Mom died to go to school in Washington D.C. where she met the man, Richard, who had such a thing about blood children. That's what he called them.

When I left for college in Flagstaff, Dad sold the house and moved into a townhouse. When he retired two years ago, he made an almost overnight move to Coronado Island. He lives in a beachfront condo he and some doctors had bought as an investment. He took over full ownership when the market fell apart in the '80s. The condo I live in now was another investment of theirs.

Dad seems happy. He travels a lot. He takes these learning tours, the ruins in Guatemala, the Greek Isles. The women on those trips must love him, he's so tall and handsome, with a full head of white hair.

When Dad's in Coronado he's going all the time. He keeps all of his plans and dates and invitations penciled in on the calendar hanging by the kitchen phone. I've seen him fretting over the empty spaces, worrying over them with a pencil in his mouth, chewing at it. What will he do? What will he do? He fills in the holes and plays golf.

He never remarried and he doesn't say much about Mom but her pictures are there on the dresser and in his study. One time when I was broken up over Baby James, crying to my daddy about how he left me, how could he do it, Dad said very quietly, "How do you think I feel, Gloria? The only thing I ever wanted in my whole life was to be married to your mother."

All those years and that was inside him and he had never said anything like it before.

"I wish I could make you happy," he told me that day. "I don't know how." Poor man.

I don't have any pictures of my mother around my condo. I do have one that was taken when she was in her early twenties. I keep it in the copy of *Gone With The Wind* I lifted from her bookshelf when I was in elementary school. It's the edition that was published after the movie with all the full-page color pictures of Vivien Leigh and Clark Gable. Every so often, every year or two, I take it out to read it again or to look at it for some reason and I am surprised when I open it and find her picture.

The picture is black and while, a professional picture with the photographer's name stamped in the corner. She is so young and pretty in the picture. Her hair is short, black and curly, the eyes are light, thick black lashes, and she has that kind of mouth that is always pouting. I wonder why it was taken.

I've never asked Dad about it but she must have been a student or even married when it was taken. Why would she want that picture, like a model? I've studied it, looking for me in her face. I have the curls in my hair and the light eyes and long eye lashes but I don't have that dark beauty. Nor does Jeanne who is the spitting image of Dad, height and all. I don't know the woman in the photograph, not at all.

She took three years to die and I never saw Dad break under the pressure, even after her death. It must have been horrible for him, a doctor, not to be able to cure the woman he loved. At the funeral he wore a black suit and acted very put together, talking to all the family who had flown in from Pennsylvania. Of course, he had all those years to prepare.

I was more stunned than sad. In the end, Jeanne and I hadn't been much a part of her dying. She spent all of her time with Dad, not us. She loved us, I know, but in the end it was all Dad. I've never talked about it much. Any problems, any depression I've had, have all come with men, not with Mom's death.

There weren't any good ones; at least, I couldn't find them. I didn't date them or feel attracted to them if they were good. Like I've told Joe, put me in a room with a bunch of good-looking men with good jobs, good educations, all nice, sweet guys, and if there is one man in there who is half drunk, scratching his crotch and belching I'll say, "Hey, that's the guy for me."

I've done it over and over again. Although in the past ten years I have consistently picked guys who had the awfulness well hidden. They have been good-looking, had the good jobs, were nice and friendly, but I always knew that underneath somewhere was a real nut case. As good as I have gotten in reading them, the better they have gotten in hiding the craziness. The drunk was the exception. He was the one scratching his butt and belching. He was, from the beginning, the obvious bum.

I told myself construction workers were like that, part of the job. It didn't occur to me or I wouldn't admit to myself that he didn't have to drink beer all day long. I put it down to the hard work he had to do in the heat and the sun.

About this time I saw Andrew again. He was in Phoenix on his way to Sedona and he called to ask me to dinner. I told him about Frank and he said to bring him along. He wanted to meet him.

Frank had been drinking even before he got to my apartment. I know now it was because he was nervous, someone out of my past and all that and it was obvious to him that Andrew and I liked each other.

At dinner he got louder and louder and

drunker and drunker. He started to talk about how he had once worked on race cars, Formula Ones. I thought, Good, now they will have something to talk about because Andrew likes racing and in Mexico we had all gone to a Formula One race. I was purring like a fat cat because my two favorite men of the moment had something in common. Sure, like oil and water.

Andrew actually rolled his eyes when he dropped us off at my apartment. This was the same apartment where one year later he chased me around the living room demanding I put on the leg warmers I wore to aerobics class. I wasn't that drunk.

"You're crazy," I yelled at him. "Some other time, Andrew."

"No, now, now," he was yelling. Finally, I gave him one of the leg warmers and pushed him out the door. Right until that moment when I shut the door he had that look of surprise on his face like, No, she isn't really not going to do this little thing for me.

I had seen that look before, when the husband of a high school friend took me home from a New Year's Eve party and made a side trip to some piece of desert where he threw himself on me and began to kiss me passionately. I pushed him off.

He kept saying, "Come on, come on, just one little kiss," and I was thinking, what is this, the 1890s? When I finally got to the apartment, he had that look on his face, that "You mean, you're really not going to do this little thing for me."

I never once saw that look on a Mexican's face.

I did lead this one Mexican on and, yes, I know that's what I was doing with Andrew and the aerobics and the leg warmers. I was the one who brought the subject up. And all the winking and blinking with the married man, showing the good legs, I did that. It didn't work so well with the Mexican. I ended up fighting a battle in a motel room, trying to explain to him in two languages that no did mean no. He had no sad little boy look on his face. He was mad, not American at all.

Makes you wonder how American mothers raise their boys. They must tease them with promises, even in a sexual way, the winking and flirting. Yes, they do it to their sons, too, not only to their husbands and their fathers and all the other men in their lives. They do it to their sons, too.

*

I have had a total of sixteen men. That's right. I have slept with only sixteen men since I started doing such things the summer after I graduated from high school and somehow it doesn't seem like a lot to me. After all, those were the '60s and '70s. The '80s were very slow.

Some of the men lasted a few months. One lasted one night. Some lasted more than a year. Some of them were worth it, most of them were not. One was wonderful. One got me pregnant. I had an abortion.

If all the American women who have had an abortion stood up, the country would be knocked on its ass, especially considering who some of them would be. They did that once in France, all the women admitting to having had an abortion. You can't shock the French but the rest of the literate world which consists of a population of about four million people in about four countries, was shocked to the point of headlines. There they were, the writers, the actresses of France, nobody else really, only the names we knew, and they all admitted to at least one abortion.

I had mine a few months before I decided to go to Mexico. The whole thing was as sad and melancholy and as draining as the relationship that caused it. Forget him. He moved to Seattle and died three years ago of stomach cancer. I heard it from a college friend in Flagstaff who keeps track of such things.

I don't think about him but I do think about the child. He would be a grown man by now although I never think of him as being much older than sixteen. It's the same way I never picture myself past the age of thirty. Sure, the baby would have been a boy. I know that. I think about him once a year or so, possibly around the same time he would have been born. I've never sat down to figure that one out and I'm not going to do it now.

I loved only one of those sixteen men. I said it to the others, that I loved them, most of them, but it was really only Baby James. Oh, how I loved Jim.

Before I loved him he said to me, "Why aren't you happy? You're healthy, have a good job, you're pretty. That's all pretty good, isn't it?"

He was a freelance photographer for the agency where I first worked when I got to Dallas and I told him I didn't know why I wasn't happy. Besides, I told him, it wasn't normal to be happy all of the time.

"I want to be," he said and for the most part he was. He was nice, happy and tall, like all my Americans. Yes, like my Dad.

He was after my second trip to Mexico. He lasted a year and then left me for a job in New York. I loved him and he loved me except for one thing.

"I am terrified of you," he told me one night. I was shocked. I demanded to know what he meant. We had been together for six months and I could barely breathe unless it was the air he had just exhaled. What the hell did he mean I terrified him?

He wouldn't tell me, refused. He closed his mouth over that one and said he wasn't going to talk about it, he couldn't.

"That was his problem" Andrew said when I told him about it. "It didn't have anything to do with you."

Now, what does that mean? Of course, it had something to do with me. He said it to me. He said it about me. Last year, one year after he left me, he married a woman in New York. A friend from the agency went to the wedding and told me the woman was fat, rude and drank too much. "The son her father never had," is what he said.

Yeah, and what does all that mean? It means he didn't want me. From me to her. From me to a fat, rude alcoholic. But I have never had any doubt about how much he did love me. I think it all comes down to the fact that the man liked being happy all of the time. He couldn't get that from me.

Now I dream of tall, handsome, Mexican men
I might meet in some small quiet town in Mexico,
some quiet beach town, some mountain town. Do
you think they are really there?

8

Of course, there is no break in the other story, no time to ruminate over lost loves or why someone still can't talk about a parent's death except to mention how well her father and sister handled it. In the middle of the other story, there is no way to lean back and wonder whether or not to go forward, whether to leave things as they are, without explanation.

Saying "And then I saw something else" is to end any hope of stopping, even if they would want you to. In fact, you give them no choice. You move quickly after that, a slight pause, then on to the finish.

"The top of the cross is coming up. It's being pulled up by ropes and as it gets higher and higher, you can see that there's a man on it." My voice gets tighter and higher. I feel physically ill, like I am going to gag on the words.

The cross has come into view, moving toward me, pulled by ropes, pushed up by hands. I see the hands lined up on the center bar, brown hands, pushing. And, on this cross, there is a man.

"There is a man on it, nailed to it and he is wearing this little loin cloth and that's all. And they are pulling up the cross with ropes or something so it's rising upright behind us. And there he is." I look up and then back at them.

Andrew says nothing. He holds his drink in both hands and looks down into it. He always shakes his head at this point, slowly, sadly. But he never says if he saw it too. In the three times we've told the story, he has never once said he saw the man hanging there.

I did.

*

No one has ever asked me what this man looked like, the man on the cross. If someone did, I don't know how I would answer. I didn't see his face, or if I did, I don't remember it. I could not tell you now if he was even a Mexican. I can't tell you how his arms looked, if his armpits were hairy or if he had heavy hair on his legs. I can't tell you if he was long and sinewy with good muscles or whether he was small or thin or white. I cannot tell you if his head had fallen forward over his chest or if he wore a crown of thorns. I know I saw all those things but I can't tell you that was the way it was, he was, because I didn't see it clearly then and I don't now.

What I did see then was Christ. I saw the Christ of every crucifix I have ever seen. I saw a movie Christ, a painted Christ, a cartoon Christ. I saw that and the cross carrying him moving up and up above me until it bisected the sky. I know the crowd behind me was moaning with mouths open, a roar of a moan. I know a hundred thousand heads stretched forward. I know it but I didn't see it.

God, it was awful. I didn't breath. I didn't moan. I didn't swallow but my eyes may have filled with tears. I don't know. I know nothing but that I was seeing him on that cross. Then the cross was straight and steady, the sky quartered by the light wood. The wood was light, I have that part right.

*

I am not a religious person. I never have been. My mother was a Catholic. She gave it her best all through Catholic schools. She went to a Catholic college and said she was finished with it after that. She would dress Jeanne and me for church every Sunday. We made our first communions and our confirmations with her in the pew but she wasn't the one who took us to church. That was Dad, the old Baptist from Texas. Mom said, "He made a promise when we got married and your Dad always keeps his promises. I already did my church duty."

Dad once told me that some of his Texas friends and friends of his family stopped talking to him because he married a Catholic but he was the one who took us to church. He had made that promise to a priest in Philadelphia, that the children of the marriage would be raised in the Church.

When we were older and when Mom got sick, Dad would drop us off at church and go home to spend Sunday morning with her. I would slide into one of the confessionals when no one was looking and spend the entire mass in there. I'd sit and think in the dark while outside they were kneeling and standing and sitting and kneeling again. I hated it out there. The church was always hot and stuffy and I didn't like having to share all that stale air with the others.

Jeanne never said a word about what I was doing. She would walk forward, finding her own place in the pews. After mass, I would meet her at the door and we would go out to find Dad waiting across the street in the car. He was keeping his promise.

We hung in a little longer after Mom died. I went to a Catholic youth group meeting once a week. At one of the meetings this priest told us that if anyone was exposed to Catholicism and did not accept it, they went to hell.

This was not some old fogey priest but a young man, as I remember him, and while I would like to picture him with soft fluttering white fingers, feminine, I don't know that to be true. He was young, too young to be saying what he did.

I thought of Dad taking us to mass every Sunday, sitting with us in that awful heat, keeping his promise. He was going to hell? Oh, I don't think so. Not my Dad. I didn't say anything though. I had tried before to question this priest and all the others in the room had turned to me, astonished.

"How dare you?" their tight little faces said. "How dare you ask a question?"

No, my lack of religion did not start with the crucifixion. That had already happened years before.

*

The only thing I can tell you about that man on the cross is that his toes were long. Isn't that strange? I don't know why I remember that, but don't all men have long toes, thin, bony? Then he did as well.

Yet, I am not all that sure I do remember his feet. I don't remember nails in them, blood, nothing. Of course, it must have registered somewhere in me, all of it had to. I was looking right at him.

What I do remember clearly, without question, is that cross being raised slowly. I remember now hearing the straining, the low grunts of the men pulling on the ropes and the men pushing up the cross from beneath. I remember the crowd moaning and I felt so goddamn sick then, like I was going to vomit.

Then, suddenly, unbelievably fast, after that one still unmoving moment when the cross was straight against the sky, it disappeared backward, the way it came. The sky was clear again except for the tops of the other two crosses framing the far corners of the hill.

The man had died.

9

I have had sixteen men, one abortion, and have seen one therapist. Not because of the thing with the nuns. That episode did bother me for years, my reaction to it, but I finally came to my own conclusions about why it happened. I realized I was a perfect candidate for a middle-of-the-night vocation, considering my situation and where I was. But in addition, and this is what I had forgotten for years, I was suffering from a horrendous hangover from drinking at a cowboy bar the night before with the photographer.

I felt bad all that next day, and guilty. What am I doing? Why am I wasting away getting drunk with some married photographer in Tucson, Arizona? Where is my life? I was into the I'm-a-mess kind of thinking. And, bang-o, it hits me. I want to be a nun. That was the tie-in I missed, the guilt and the hangover. I don't think any therapist would have gotten to that faster than I did.

My friend Trish has seen a number of them. From what she's told me and what I've seen with her, they don't seem to tie things together well. She'll have a problem because she can't breakup with a man who is nuts and her psychiatrist is talking to her about why her father had a drinking problem because of her grandfather.

I met Trish at one of the agencies I write for in

Dallas. She does some modeling between the college classes she's taking to become a paralegal. She has been married once and has had two abortions because she forgot to use her diaphragm. Nice. At one point in the '80s she was using cocaine although no one was supposed to know. She never admitted she was using but used to make these strange four-o'clock-in-the-morning phone calls to me. She is tall, blond, blue-eyed and very pretty. We do tend to forgive pretty people many things.

During those phone calls she would ask me, "Didn't you ever use cocaine, Gloria?" I'd always say the same thing, that I hadn't and had no desire to.

I didn't know Trish when I decided to see a therapist but if I had, I doubt I would have asked her for a recommendation. I found mine in the telephone book and chose him because he would see me within a week and his office was close to my condo.

When I first got there, I saw this short fat man running around the reception area. He had long greasy hair and his shirttail was untucked. I thought, No, this can't be him. Hold back on the negative first impressions.

Of course it was him. Right off the bat he wanted to know how much my insurance was going to cover. Then he started talking about all the tests he needed to do, the chemical breakdowns, blood tests. He told me how he was writing a book on how the size of the feet could be an indication of certain mental problems. I'm not kidding.

He looked down at my feet and said, "You

have small feet." I told him I was relatively small all over. I was thinking that this guy was definitely crazier than I could ever be and he also had dandruff.

He wasn't stupid though. Within the first few minutes he said, "You aren't coming back, are you?"

No, I was not.

"Well, you know what's best," he said.

Now, if he had said that with a sneer, it would have made more sense. That would have been the psychiatrist kind of thing, a way of pointing out how much you really did need help and how you were running away from your problems and how he knew it. But this man said it with a sad little voice, like nothing ever turned out right for him. And there it was again, that sad look of Andrew's and the married man, that Oh-you-really-aren't-going-to-let-me-do-what-I-want look.

I was laughing out loud by the time I got out of his office. I was laughing because of him and because I felt so sane in comparison. Small feet, please.

Why him at all? Well, I was trying to figure out why I was yelling at everyone, at cashiers, waiters, people in the post office. One day I stood in the middle of the condo parking lot and screamed at some old woman who was parking her car in my reserved space.

"Who the hell do you think you are? It says reserved!" I yelled, pointing toward the sign. "Get your car out of there, you stupid old woman." Then I went into the condo and burst into tears.

I had been in Dallas for a year, working for an agency again and trying to find another job. I was miserably unhappy. I knew no one in town but Joe and Becky. I went back to Phoenix whenever I had enough money or time, which wasn't often, but outside of Dad, there wasn't anything there for me either.

Every morning I had to grit my teeth before I could walk through the front door of the agency. I had to share my office with a copy writer I couldn't stand. Since the day I arrived, I had to listen to him making phone calls looking for work outside of Dallas. That was all he ever talked about, his job search and how great his work was and how no one could appreciate it in this cow town.

This one morning he was gushing all over the phone to someone about his endless search for the job in the big city, New York, Chicago, L.A. He was telling him his work was too good for Dallas, that he was out there on the cutting edge of advertising, whatever that means, that his last ad was going to win a national award or should if those people in New York didn't have their heads up their asses.

I knew the ad well, the idea for it had been mine, a fact he never mentioned to the person on the other end of the line, or to me, or to anyone else as far as I knew.

He hung up and I looked at him and said, "You know, I've never liked you." I said it in a perfectly flat, calm way and he looked at me in total shock.

This was the same man who made such a to-do about my birthday a few months before. He had insisted on taking me out to a birthday lunch at a French restaurant and handing me a rose and a card when I got into his car.

"Nope," I said, "I never liked you." It felt great to say it. I felt relieved. I wasn't about to stop. I told him how he always took credit for everyone else's ideas, how he was always asking for help but never acknowledging where he got the ideas. The ad he was so hot on was perfect proof. I had been the one who suggested that he take a look at the old car ads, the ones in the '20s and '30s with the long sleek cars and the sleek women in front of them. I said he might do a take-off on that concept. I told him to take a look at the magazines from that period, to check out a few books from the library. I even told him which ones.

I gave him the starting point but he ended up developing his whole presentation using the old ads. The campaign required the creativity of a doorknob. He went to the library, brought a few books into the office and basically copied the ads with help of the art director.

But this is what he said to me that day I told him what I really thought of him. "I came up with that car campaign," he said. "You didn't have anything to do with it. It was my idea. You may have mentioned old cars but anyone could have done that."

No, I told him. That isn't what happened. I gave him the idea, as I had done before. I told him where to go, where to look. I gave him the idea and he didn't even have enough creativity to take it one step forward. He didn't have any ideas, I told him, and those he did have weren't any good. I told him that was why he wasn't getting any job offers.

"You're not creative," I told him. "They can see that. They can see you copy other people's work, dead people, for that matter. You don't come up with new ideas. Even the thing you think is your best idea is from sixty years ago. That's why you aren't getting a job in New York. That's the real reason."

That had to get to him because he had already decided why he wasn't getting hired by one of the big agencies in New York. He had a whole list of reasons and none of them had anything to do with his work. He told me over and over again, and all the people he talked to on the phone, that he wasn't getting the jobs because he wasn't Jewish or because he didn't go to the right schools, the right colleges, because his family was blue collar, and why shouldn't they be proud of it, because he was in Texas and nobody hired anybody from Texas. No, it had nothing to do with the fact that someone might think his work was less than great.

He said nothing as I was going through my tirade. When I finally stopped talking he said, "Did you know it was my birthday last week?" Yes, I did know and I had chosen to ignore it. He got up and left the room.

God, who could blame him? The bitch of the world. I didn't like being that way. I could have let him go on and on with the phone calls and the excuses. Who asked me to be the great truth teller?

I was doing too much of this, this yelling, truth telling, blowing up at people who had simply moved into my range. I was a loose cannon. I was ready to explode, was exploding all over the place. I needed help. That's how I ended up with a therapist I saw for fifteen minutes. But first, the day after the tirade, I had to apologize.

"Sorry," I said, "I was having a bad day." And I told him I knew that wasn't any excuse for saying what I did.

He accepted that. "Okay," he said. "It happens." But he wasn't going to let it go, not all of it. He said, "But you didn't mean what you said about my work, that it wasn't good. You didn't mean that, did you?"

I couldn't stop myself.

"Oh yeah," I said. "I meant that." Then I pushed past him and went out to get a cup of coffee. So much for apologies.

Later I heard he left advertising and went to work for a small magazine in San Francisco, writing articles about what's new in computers. I didn't care about him then and I don't care about him now. I did care about those outbursts of mine. They were too angry even if they were right.

Obviously the psychiatrist wasn't going to help. What did help was a conversation with the photographer the agency used. I was telling him about this therapist who was crazy and he said, "You know that angry thing you were talking about, that yelling at people for no reason? It sounds like you just needed someone to listen to you. That's why you were yelling, nobody was listening."

He said, "The stupidest thing you did in all of this was going to a shrink. What for? What was he supposed to tell you, that you were wrong to be angry that nobody was listening to you? That's not crazy. You should be angry. Why are you beating yourself up?"

Good question.

That was Baby James, Jim, Jimmy. We didn't start dating until a couple of years later but I always had a soft spot for him. He was great, positive about everything. I trusted him. I told him about the abortion, about how I lost my virginity, everything. I told him how dumb I'd been about men like Paul and Frank, the drunk.

Frank was a classic. I denied his problem for months. The guy was a knee-crawling drunk and I'm saying to myself, "Oh, that's just the way he is, on vacation, resting."

I finally had to admit there was a problem the night I watched him sneak out to his car four or five times to take a swig from a bottle of booze I wouldn't have drunk from if I was dying of thirst. He didn't know I could see him through the kitchen window. He also had a six-pack of beer inside the apartment but he still needed those other trips. Yes, a little problem there.

For a while I tried to keep up with him. He drank, I drank. The fighting finally got to me, the accusations that there was something wrong with me, I was flirting, being obnoxious. One of Trish's friends listened to me go on about him and said, "Oh, yeah, a drunk." This guy was a recovering alcoholic and suggested I check out an AA meeting if I had any doubts. That's why I went to a meeting right after that bad fight.

The next day I said to Frank, "You know, I think you have a drinking problem."

"Maybe I do," he said. "But what about you?"

What about me?

I'll say this for Frank, he could make me laugh and he was a good listener, like James. With both of them I felt free enough to talk about myself and things I had done, the stupid things, the things that had hurt me. But I never told either of them about the crucifixion.

I don't talk about it, not like that. I've never told my sister, my father, any of the men I've dated. It only comes up, except for those three other times, when Andrew and I are together.

Maybe it is some kind of penance, that we are paying back for being there that day and we have to keep coming back to the story until our penance is done. I know that sounds melodramatic but it's a hangover from my Catholic days. Still, we must have done something wrong because I sincerely doubt the others who were there that day keep coming back to the story the way we do.

Of course, even those who climbed the first mountain, even Cynthia and Ricardo, didn't end up where we did, didn't see what we saw and didn't end up running the way we had to.

Paul and I never talked about it and I doubt he talks about it now. He has probably forgotten all about it. I might have too if it weren't for Andrew.

Becky and Joe did bring it up once. They had something to remember. Becky was beaten with sticks on their way back down the road. Men chased her and hit at her legs with sticks. Joe was walking behind her and he was walking real slow and being real quiet.

"I wasn't going to stop 'em," he told me that night in Dallas. "They would have killed me. Those morons wanted somethin' to die."

And, God knows, it wasn't going to be Joe.

10

"Did you ever think I would be this successful?" Joe once asked me as he floated around his
swimming pool.

This was his idea of success, the pool, the
floating plastic chair, a beer in one hand, the sunglasses, the stereo system that fed out to the backyard. He had it made, no question about it. He had
married Becky, stepped into her father's trucking
business. He had become a true Texan, this Polish
boy from Indiana, short, stocky, loud and happy.

Becky and Joe had three children, spaced three
years apart. Becky kept the big house with the help
of a Mexican maid, the big yard with the help of a
Mexican gardener, the pool with the help of a pool
company. In her spare time, and there didn't seem
to be much of it between telling everyone what to
do and driving the kids to fifteen activities a day,
she bred red chow dogs in the backyard kennels.

They had the house in Dallas, a time-share
condo in Vail. They belonged to a country club so
Joe could entertain clients, whatever clients there
might be for a trucking company. Joe was right.
They were, in every sense of the word, a success.
My mother would have said they were both nice
people. Possibly.

I reconnected with them a few years after
Nixon left office. The reason I remember it that way

is because of a fight we got into over him. They were living in a smaller house then. The big money and big success didn't hit until the '80s but they had already begun their upward movement.

None of this was new to Becky. Her family had always had a piece of the blue collar pie, the kind of money made by a few men who worked with their hands as well as their brains. Her dad had started out as a truck driver. He ended up owning the biggest trucking company in Texas, or something like that.

She was still pretty, that first time I saw them after Mexico. She was that dimpled, sweet-talking Texas woman, friendly and hospitable, all a winkin' and a blinkin'. My Dad had a couple of aunts like that, except when they thought you weren't looking, they'd get this mean look on their faces, real tight around the mouth. Becky would start getting that look too as she got older. Ain't easy being sweet all the time.

I think I had stopped in Dallas after visiting the relatives in Pennsylvania. Joe asked me to spent the night with them. We drank our way through dinner with friends of theirs and at some point Joe started to talk about the crucifixion. Except for that one phone call from Andrew a few years before, I hadn't thought about it once.

Joe didn't have much of a story to tell. He and Becky never made it to either the mountain or the field. They'd spent most of their time climbing up the road, trying to figure out what was going on and then going back down the road to the cars. I let him tell how these crazy Mexicans were going to crucify some guy.

"So when we're walking back to town these guys start hittin' Becky's legs with sticks," he tells the friends, "but I wasn't gonna do a thing. I didn't even look at 'em. I just kept walkin' like I didn't know who she was. Shit, those fuckers would have killed me if I made a move. They would have killed me. Those morons wanted somethin' to die."

At this point, I looked up and said, very quietly, "The man did die, you know. The man who was crucified, he died."

I thought they knew that, that we all knew. Hadn't we talked about it at the party later? They must have known that part. But they both turned on me.

"He did not, Gloria," they yelled at me.

"You're crazy," Becky said and Joe said to his friends, "She exaggerates, always did."

"He did die," I tried telling them again. "You didn't see what we saw," but Joe was hooting with laughter and Becky's eyes were narrowed and she kept saying, "You're so crazy, Gloria." I shut up and said nothing else about it.

The friends left and we kept drinking. Something got us on to politics and I laughed and said I was always shocked that anyone with half a brain could have voted for Nixon. I said all you had to do was watch the man on television and you knew he was a liar and half-crazed. Look at his eyes, I said. They always flew all over the place when he talked. They did.

"Well, then, you must think we are really stupid," Becky says in this tight little voice, her teeth clenched. "We voted for him. We must be stupid, right?"

It had never occurred to me that anyone I knew or had ever been friends with could have voted for this man, and even if they had, they wouldn't have admitted it. Nobody did. Not then. Even in Arizona, most people were still too embarrassed to say they had anything to do with putting him in office. Not at Becky's house, they weren't embarrassed there.

The conversation went straight downhill, from Nixon to Kennedy, both John and Ted. They hated them both. Ted was a drunk and a murderer and John got us into Viet Nam. Didn't I know that and wasn't it Nixon who got us out? That one came from Becky.

I couldn't say anything. Everything I said was dumb. What was I, some kind of hippy? Yuck, yuck. That came from Joe. A liberal? What? They didn't stop. They kept laughing at me and attacking me, both of them, a team.

I hadn't expected it, not from them. None of us argued in Mexico, not about politics. We never talked about them. We never cared. I wasn't a hippy in the '70s. I didn't demonstrate. I was living in California. I was either at my job or at the beach, not much else. Then I moved back to Phoenix where I worked and took classes to finish my degree. I was against the war, sure, and vocal about it, and I was against Nixon but who had the time for politics?

By now that meanness was really showing on Becky's face. Her face was contorted with a kind of hate I couldn't even begin to understand. Why was she so angry at me? She said something about how we could have won the war if it weren't for all those "dirty hippy commies." Joe was yelling that I never knew what I was talking about, never. They seemed absolutely united in this dislike of me, Becky with that tight little mouth and Joe with his yelling.

"Fucking bleeding-heart liberals lost that one for us. They killed more Americans in Viet Nam than the Cong did," is what he said. People did talk that way then. They still do.

"So, why didn't you go?" I asked him and I could see Becky puff up at the audacity of my asking him that.

"I was married," he yelled at me, but as drunk as I was I could still see he knew it wasn't all that great of an answer. First of all, he didn't have to get married to stay out and second, I, for one, knew he wasn't all that excited about getting married. He had called Paul and me in Tennessee.

"Should I marry her?" he wanted to know. I didn't have an answer and I didn't know why he was asking me.

"Do you want to? Do you have to?" I asked him. "Is she pregnant or something?"

She wasn't.

"Well, if you want to, go ahead," I told him. Why was he asking me this? I had no interest at all in what he did.

"Fucker wants to make goddamn sure he stays out of Viet Nam," is what Paul said later. "He'll have her knocked up in a week, if she isn't already. Besides, the old man is loaded. Why not marry her?" Why not, indeed.

I didn't remind Joe about that phone call the night of the fight and I've never brought it up in all the times I've been with them since and the few times I've let myself get into another argument with them. Those times have been accidents or when I couldn't keep my mouth shut one second longer. But as a rule, when I was seeing them, I said nothing much about anything.

I made the move from Arizona in the mid '80s. I needed the change. I could make more money here than in Scottsdale. The weather made more sense, fewer 110-degree days. You also get tired of living near your old hometown, and Scottsdale and Phoenix were rapidly becoming one city. Anyway, with Dad being a Texan, I was acceptable in Dallas.

The first few years here, I saw a lot of Joe and Becky. I spent the holidays with them when I couldn't get back to Phoenix. I called Becky at least once a week to see if she wanted to take a break from the kids and the chows to have lunch or hit a movie. She seldom did. We never connected, she and I. I finally realized the only thing we did have in common was that time in Mexico and we weren't all that close down there. The consensus was that Becky had come down to find an American husband and when she found one, she took him home.

I haven't seen them at all in the past year and Becky has never called to find out why. Same town and not one phone call in one year. I was interested to see how long it might take her. Now I know.

That part doesn't bother me, the Becky part, but Joe is a different matter. I always liked Joe. He could always make me laugh. He cared about me in Mexico, the way a big brother would.

One night after Paul had been particularly rotten, Joe told me he would never speak to me again if I followed Paul to Tennessee. He said he would wash his hands of me if I did that. I did and he didn't.

There was another drunken night at their house when he told me he too had a bit of a crush on me in Mexico and he couldn't figure out why I never saw it.

"I thought you'd get tired of Paul and turn around and see me standing there. That's what I thought but you never did." That's what he said.

Now, what am I supposed to do with that piece of information twenty years later?

The answer I gave him that day when he was lolling around in the pool wondering whether or not I ever thought he would be that successful was, "I never thought much about it, Joe."

That was true. I had never thought about success one way or the other. In Mexico I didn't measure success by pools in backyards or by anything else for that matter. I didn't think about success in Mexico. Did they?

If I thought about the future in Mexico, it was that I would travel, enjoy myself, maybe finish school somewhere in the U.S. I didn't think about marriage or children. I didn't have a dream of what life was going to be or could be. I had no immediate goals. I thought things were going to keep on in the same way, the same pattern, the same rhythm.

Success for me was certainly never a swimming pool in the backyard. A lot of people I knew already had one. or I thought they did. Paul didn't, as it turned out, but then I figured we would have the whole Pacific Ocean.

11

This must seem like the end, for the listeners, the winding down of the story. The man has died. It was unexpected, horrible, and that's the end. They're sitting there in shock, their eyes wide, mouths hanging open. I don't think they expect much more. They certainly can't expect the story to get worse but we are not finished yet.

"Then from down below us, from the road below us, these four men come running up the hill carrying a stretcher," Andrew tells them. "It's a canvas stretcher with poles." He makes two fists as though grabbing the poles at the end of the stretcher.

"They're carrying it up, right past us." He looks to one side. "Remember?" He turns back to me and I nod, never talking my eyes from his face.

"First they come up right past us and then a second later they come back down and there's a body on it." I am nodding with his words.

"They have covered it with a blanket," he tells them, "but we can see it because it's right there, right next to us." He motions to one side.

"The crowd opened up," I say then, going back to the appearance of the stretcher, "and this stretcher came up from the middle of it and right past us."

Now Andrew is nodding.

"That was the thing," I say. "Everything was

right next to us." It is important that they understand this, as important as the fact the man died. Everything that happened, the cross going up on the hill, the man on it, the stretcher, was right next to us.

Andrew nods and takes it back. "These four guys carrying the stretcher are wearing some kind of military uniform, helmets, boots, the whole thing. I don't know why they were. Everybody in Mexico has some kind of uniform. But they weren't Red Cross. They were probably there to keep the peace.

"You can see the man on the stretcher had to be dead because they have this blanket or this sheet pulled over his face."

Here is where I stiffen with the memory. Here is where my mouth goes dry and ugly. Say it, Andrew, say what it is that I saw that makes me sick and gag with the memory of it. But he doesn't, not all of it.

He tells them, "The thing is, and this was bad, one of the hands has fallen outside of the blanket and it's hanging off the stretcher as they run by."

But, Andrew, that's not all. Why don't you say what I saw, what still makes my face contort with the horror of it. I can't say it. I never have, not to any listener. But it makes me as sick now as it did that day. I want to gag and rub my face and dig my nails into my forehead and pull my hands down until my face is empty again, flat. I saw something more.

As they pass, this huffing and puffing quartet of small men, all the same size, all dressed in brown and beige, as they pass, I see the hand hanging down from the stretcher and there is blood pouring from it. And I see more. I see the hole in the palm of his hand. I see the hole. And this, of everything else, is what I will never, never forget. I see the hole in his hand.

*

Oh, they want it over, want it done. There has to be an ending to this, they must be thinking. But the pacing doesn't change. There is no letdown, no slowing. If anything, we are moving faster, breathing faster.

"Then the priest starts talking over the loud-speaker system," Andrew says. "I didn't understand much of it but you speak better Spanish, Gloria. You tell them what he was saying." My turn again.

"He said that this wasn't supposed to happen. He doesn't say what it was that happened but everyone knows the guy is dead. The priest is saying that this man is only a symbol of what Christ did for us. That sort of thing. He said they all needed to understand that, that this was only a symbol of Christ's sacrifice."

"Why?" the listeners ask. They want to know why the priest said anything, why he said that in particular, what he meant. They don't ask the full questions. The look on their faces shows what they mean. They are confused, almost angry. Oh yes, the little story has gone on too long.

"Because the people don't understand what's going on," says Andrew.

"No," I correct him, "they're getting mad now. See, the man wasn't supposed to die, not this way.

"He didn't hang up there long enough," I say with a knowing smile. "That's what they wanted to see, him up there on the cross, but he was up there only for a second."

They are angry now, the listeners. I can see it in their faces. They are angry and frustrated. They want one of us to explain why any of this happened. We don't give them time to ask their questions and I doubt they could find the right words if we did. I doubt they could admit they are angry at us, not for that day, but for what we are doing to them now.

"It got very frightening," Andrew says quietly. "You could sense there was going to be trouble, a riot perhaps. You could feel it coming."

"And who do you think they see standing all alone in the middle of this field?" I ask them, and when I ask, when it starts hitting home why our position in the field is so important to the story, I am back in control. The emotions are gone, the story becomes everything again.

"They see three white people standing alone in their field while the priest is telling them nobody is to blame for this, that none of it was supposed to happen."

"And there we were," says Andrew.

"So, they decide to blame us," I say.

The listeners react in horror. Again, they demand the answer. "Why would they blame you? You haven't done anything."

"Because we're white and because he wasn't

up there long enough," I tell them.

"Now we have a problem," Andrew says and leans forward to the listeners. At this moment, when he leans to them, hands clasped, elbows resting on his knees, he becomes the lawyer again, the older man, discussing an interesting case history with equally sophisticated and educated friends, lawyer friends and their wives.

"Now," he reminds them, "we have to get back down the hill." The story is his again. I will add the color but only after he has set the stage.

"So we started back for the cars," he says, "and all of these people are lining the road. They watch us walk down from the field and then start walking down the road. You could see they wanted to get mad at somebody, like they had been cheated out of something."

"A fiesta, a party," I say.

"Yes," he agrees.

I have to tell the listeners the way they looked, these people, because Andrew doesn't.

"They are all standing along the road and they are swaying back and forth, from side to side, like animals do." I make a soft swaying movement to show them how it was. "And they are watching us as we walk past them."

Andrew nods but I don't know if he really remembers that. I don't think anyone could but me. I don't think anyone looked into those empty brown eyes but me. It was so strange. They stared but I don't think they saw us. They were all trying to figure out what had happened. Then men started breaking away from the crowd and moving in behind us on the road.

"Don't walk fast," Andrew told me, "and don't look back."

I thought, as I had with Ricardo, that it was because of my light eyes, that he didn't want them to see my blue eyes. But now I think it was the same warning we give when we know someone who is crazy is watching us or only looking at us. "Don't meet their eyes," we say. "Don't look at them." And, this time, I don't look back.

"They started to chase us," says Andrew. "First they are walking with us or behind us and then they start to move in, to crowd us. It was terribly frightening. I didn't think we were going to make it out of there without somebody being hurt."

I say then, "Joe and Becky told me they were halfway down the hill when people started going for them."

"Really?" He says this each time.

I explain to the audience. "Becky is this white, white blond and Joe is this tough little Polish guy. He's blondish but not like Becky. They both were obviously American. Joe told me that people were hitting Becky's legs with sticks and that he fell back and acted like he didn't care what was going on because he figured he'd be dead if he tried to stop them."

"They would have hurt him," Andrew agrees, "but I don't know if they would have killed him.

"Now, if we had started to run, I don't know what they would have done," he adds. "You can't run in a situation like that. You keep walking straight ahead. You don't look at anybody."

Here he wipes at his forehead, rubs it. "It could have been bad, very, very, bad. I was just waiting to feel a knife between my ribs. I thought it could happen."

We didn't run on the road but we did run when we reached the town. I was yelling, "Go to the church. We have to go to the church." Paul and Andrew were running with me or ahead of me or behind me. I don't remember where they were but I remember running into the church. A few of the Mexicans who had been chasing us ran in after us and then bunched up at the door, trying to decide if they should follow us all the way in.

I am vague about this part, about the church. I feel as though something else happened before we got there, something in the street, against the church wall. Someone being thrown against it, something like that. Or that might have been before all of this, when we first got to the town and saw the parade.

I remember that, the parade and all the priests ringing their bells and swinging the incense holders. They were all dressed with lace over their cassocks. There was also a stage there in an empty field or lot. There was a long table on it. I suppose it was for the part of the passion play about the Last Supper. That is what it looked like, this long empty table on that wooden stage. Or maybe it was an altar.

It is as though I dreamed it all, those little brown priests in their yellow and pink lace petticoats. Yellow and pink, is that possible?

So there was a parade and the altar and the

church. I remember the church but as if it were in a dream and it is never part of the story. Andrew takes the story directly back to the cars. Then we go back to the city.

What did happen in there was that we all ran in, even those Mexicans, and then Andrew and Paul and I sat down and tried to catch our breath. We may have been laughing between gasps. We laughed and talked but not about the crucifixion, about something else. Who knows what it might have been, something like, "What a day." But, if I have the picture right, we were all sitting in the front pew under some statue with the candles blazing around it and we were laughing.

12

I do know the times I have told the story alone, I have felt a secret smile cross my face. I always recognize that smile on other people's faces. I saw it once on the face of a temporary friend who had just finished telling me how horrible her husband was, how he had cheated on her, how he was stupid, drank too much, took her money. I was appalled, had to be. She had fed me dinner and wine and I seemed to be her only friend in Dallas. I felt free to offer advice right and left, nodding, stomping about, banging my fist on the table.

"You have to do this and that," I told her. "This is a nightmare. You don't have to put up with this."

There I was, all worked up and irate over what she'd been going through and the bastard who was ruining her life when I saw it, that tiny wisp of a smile on her face as she reached for her coffee cup. It was that secret smile, almost a smirk, that she had done well, told this little story, turned all the attention to herself. She looked, at that moment, as though she had just stolen the candy and lied enough to get her brother slapped. It's a mean little smile.

That's the smile I've felt on my face after telling the story alone. Why do I tell it alone? I don't like myself when I start the telling and I don't like myself when I am finished. I don't know why I do it.

Why does Andrew? Why does he always tell the story with me and always to some new woman. You can always see by the look on their faces that no matter how long they've been together, how close they are, he has never mentioned any of it before. He may never have mentioned that he was even in Mexico.

Don't you find that strange? It would be like finding out your boyfriend was in the helicopter when they were pushing Viet Cong out for laughs at 1,000 feet. He never says anything, doesn't seem to suffer because of it but one night he chooses to tell the story at some dinner party. Why do it that way? How much could it matter to him if that's the way he tells you? And then, after he is finished, you are supposed to go into dinner and talk about something else. I would certainly wonder about that man and his reasons.

Of course, we've got a whole country full of people telling other people horrible stories about themselves, highly personal things, the kind of story you should only want to share with someone you trust or who you want to trust. I've been sucked in at least once by that sort of confession, someone sharing a very personal experience with me and me thinking that made me special to him.

I was at a business luncheon sitting next to a man who worked for a local bank. I had spoken to him before and thought he was attractive. At this lunch, he leaned close to me and out of nowhere he started to tell me how his parents had committed suicide when he was a boy. He told me they went into the garage, shut the door and turned on the car.

"Whatever the reasons," he said, "they wanted to be together. And, they were right. They wouldn't have been worth a shit without each other."

My God, I was shocked speechless. I couldn't breathe. My mouth must have been hanging open. Not only that he had to live with this but that he should share it with me. I was stunned but I was also touched and knew he needed me to respond in some way. Why else would he have told me? I fell in love at that moment. What a good, trusting man.

I mooned over him, the thought of him. I spoke to other people about him, told them what a caring and gentle man he must be. I told my friend Trish that this man had told me something terribly personal but I wasn't free to discuss it, something given to me in confidence. What a good man and such pretty eyes and such stature. He was tall, another one of my Americans.

A couple of weeks later and this highly personal, gently entrusted story of family history appears in the local business journal. My good man had written a column on the need for local business support for community self-help groups. One of the reasons he gave was that, "Not everyone who commits suicide is either very young or very old or alone." After all, he told them, his own parents had committed suicide in the front seat of a Chevrolet, engine running, garage door locked.

"People do that, you know," was his closing

line. What bothered me was the way he used the story. He didn't say a suicide hotline might have helped them or that they looked for help but couldn't find it. Everything else about the article was very businesslike, the benefits business can derive from being part of the community, the need for involvement. Then, here comes this zinger out of nowhere with a last line that was more snide than anything else. What was the point?

I was more shocked reading that column than I was when he leaned over and told me the story. The suicide of his parents was apparently something he took out and flashed at me, at the newspaper, at everyone. All the people I had told about how kind and gentle this man was, I now told about how he had put his story in the paper, the thing I thought was so personal, and for no apparent reason.

"You're kidding," they all said.

I don't know if they really understood why I was so angry. Most of them were too surprised by what had happened to his parents. But for me that column meant I wasn't special to him. I was only another audience.

I too have been guilty of using the story, but I've chosen my audience and have only told it three times by myself. The third time the listener wasn't a man so any theory that I am interested in the men I tell the story to is wrong. I wasn't interested in this woman either. I hated her.

She was one of the people I started working for when I went freelance with the agencies. I was working for twenty-five dollars an hour back then and her agency was charging the clients seventy-five for my services. I knew what they were doing but I needed the money and this way I didn't have to be in an office eight hours a day every day.

Lydia used me a lot. Her assignments were always confusing, the information she gave me was always incorrect. She would make promises to clients without telling me, set deadlines that couldn't be met. I took the money and kept my mouth shut until this one day.

As was her style, she had invited me for lunch at a chi-chi Dallas restaurant she believed she had discovered. She sat there babbling on and on about her life and loves and successes and problems. She was one of those women who believe nothing in your life could possibly be as interesting, as important, as what went on in theirs. I don't think she was aware I had any kind of life outside of the time I spent with her or doing her work.

I was tired of Lydia and her babbling. I wanted to shock her, upset her little world of dingle-dangle bracelets and long, red, enameled fingernails and perfect lipstick line. So I trotted out the story.

I performed for her, using all the words and the actions, all the body movement to describe the opening of the little boy's head, the opening of the crowd to spit out the stretcher, the swaying of the empty-eyed people on the road.

This was a cheap version of the way Andrew and I do it, arms flailing around, shoulders shaking, awful. It was the last time I told the story and the last time I worked for Lydia.

She didn't say much of anything but she stared

at me as though I was sick and one of the things I saw in her eyes that day in the restaurant was fear, fear of me. That makes me sad.

13

The ending of this story is that Andrew is successful and Republican. Joe and Becky are successful and Republican. Anyone else who was there that day is Republican. I'm not Republican. I'm not much of anything. I am certainly not successful.

I am poor. The car is old, the one-bedroom condo is Dad's. The credit cards are gone, destroyed with trying to stay alive in the '80s. I am still putting together press kits for agencies and they are still underpaying me and overcharging their clients. I still say okay because I need time to work on the screenplay which may or may not be done before I am dead.

Once a month or maybe twice, I put on the high heels and the pantyhose and head into the high-rises with the copy I have written or for a lunch with someone who can throw some work my way. The money is always tight, always, and there are some nights when I wake up and stare at the ceiling and wonder what will become of me and my dreams.

The dreams are down to two. One is going back to Mexico, living in a small town, writing my screenplay. But then the reality hits, I am on the wrong side of forty with no steady income, no future.

I remember watching Becky spend thirty dollars for a pair of Italian shoes on sale in Mexico. Today I watch Trish spend one hundred and twenty dollars for a pair of shoes. The feeling is the same. I have no money for those things and probably never will, but I should.

I worry about things like health insurance and car insurance and disability insurance. We've reached a point in this country where we are spending our time worrying about how we can afford all the insurance we have to have to stay alive. I've reached a point where I can't even have a dream about going back to Mexico because I have to think about insurance. What happens if I get sick down there?

Thinking like that frightens me because it makes me feel like this is the end, a condo in Dallas, Texas. What the hell am I doing in Dallas, Texas?

I used to think I would travel forever, move from one exciting place to another, picking up friends and adventures along the way. I supposed I did, in a small way. I moved around a bit after Mexico but no place exciting, Phoenix, California, Scottsdale, Dallas. I've thought about backtracking a bit, back to Arizona, maybe Tucson or maybe northern California along the coast or maybe move to New Mexico. Maybe not.

I am too old for Mexico, I guess. I won't be the pretty señorita anymore down there. I won't be able to glide through the marketplace with everyone knowing me and calling out to me. Instead, I will be the nutty old gringa in the shack, pecking away on an old laptop and gumming her food.

And women like me are a joke in Mexico, like the two face lifts on the bus. The men don't want them, not the rich ones. Even if I do have a few more good years, Mexico would be tough. You have to have something to do down there after the first couple of months, something real. In the end, I would always want to come back home.

That's the strange part, that I have never been able to get that far from home. I think it's a sickness, like living in Dallas, Texas. Being a white, middle-class, not-yet-old American, is like an addiction. It's so easy, just sit back and take your shot. You let it all roll over you, the politicians, the looters in their Brooks Brothers suits, the poor sleeping in the parks, the cop beatings, the rapes, the dope, the little wars we have every few years. Go home, lock your doors, turn on your TV and shoot up. We've all given up, all of us. We don't have any dreams left. I gave up when I came back that second time, when I came back here.

To me, this country is one big sanitarium, the whole place, one big hospital for the mentally tired as well as the completely crazy. We all have our little chores in the hospital, our jobs, our crafts, the things that keep us busy until we die. We are safe, protected and nothing terrible or exciting is ever going to happen to us. If you are white, relatively attractive and have an education, you only have to sit back, do the minimum amount of work and the money comes in. Not great money necessarily, but enough.

And if you want more, if you are a white male from the perfect white college, if you work hard, step on faces, lie, cheat, steal, smile, you will make a fortune and never be happy. You will, however, have lots of things and be almost forever protected.

The only thing our hospital cannot protect us from is death and we are appalled by that. We are so appalled that when death comes we have to sue someone. How dare they let us die? We aren't supposed to die, we Americans.

You know, I did know a boy who died in Viet Nam. I forget that sometimes. I was in high school and he had been part of our crowd the summer before he joined the Marines. He was a nice enough guy who didn't have to join. Viet Nam was only heating up and none of us knew anything about it.

We all went to the funeral. That part wasn't bad. The awful part was the coffin. Kerry, the girl who married the guy who jumped me in the desert, was the one who pointed it out as the pallbearers carried the coffin out of the church. She was the smart one, always saying out loud what we had missed.

She pinched me hard and said, "It's too short. Look at it. It's too short."

The coffin was too short. Brian had been almost six foot five. He wouldn't have fit into this coffin.

"They sent him back without his head," she said. Maybe so. The story was he had been decapitated by a helicopter blade but I don't know whether that came up after the funeral or before and it may have been Kerry's story. But, even now, the only thing I remember about Brian is his coffin.

There have been other deaths, of course, my

mother, my grandparents whom I never knew or don't remember, but they haven't affected me much. I'm not afraid of dying myself. I suppose the worst thing will be the fighting for the last breath, which I will do, and seeing some doctor in front of me with short dark hair, wearing a white coat and staring back at me. I doubt there will be anyone else there, if there should be anyone at all.

That's what we're really afraid of, isn't it, dying alone, which is the reality of death. I don't care who else is in the room. We die alone and frightened and nobody can make a difference or protect us from it. That's why men dying in war call for their mothers, not out of love but for protection. She was supposed to protect them from this. They weren't supposed to die knowing that dying was what they were doing. Where was she to stop this?

I don't know if I'll call for my mother with my last breath. I think I'll just feel sad about the whole damn thing. Besides, so often in my life I have felt as though I was just treading water, waiting to die. I think, in part, this country makes me feel that way.

Mexico was life to me. I came alive down there. I could breathe again on that second trip, not those tight little breaths I took in Scottsdale, but normal, deep, good breaths. Yet three months later I was back on the plane to Arizona and my little job and my little future. I can't get away from being a patient.

I heard a guy crying on the radio last night, that deep man-sobbing that makes you catch your breath. He was a new citizen and he loved this country.

"It's a crazy and wonderful country," he said and then he went into a long empty hole of silence. The talk show host said nothing, let the hole stand unfilled until the new citizen spoke again.

"A whole lot of crazy," he said, his voice breaking, "but a whole lot of wonderful."

All of the air came out of me with that and I cried as I drove my car. I didn't cry because what he said was true but because of how much this country meant to him. That's why I cried, because he felt that way. To me, the wonderfulness is that we still feel that way about this country. The awfulness is that it is simply no longer true.

I know what the Republicans think, Joe and Becky and Andrew. It all worked for them. They have what they want, what they deserve. If other people in this country or anywhere else don't, that's their own fault. Joe and Becky certainly aren't going to give away anything that they've got and Andrew is afraid somebody is going to come and take some of his. He thinks it is going to be somebody from Mexico or Guatemala or Nicaragua. He used to think it would be somebody from Cuba.

He used to feel we should invade all of those countries down there, control them because they were all going to turn communist. He turned into one of those people who thought anything, anyone was better than a movement toward Communism, any dictator with reflector sunglasses and five billion dollars in American banks, any army that tortured prisoners with the electric cattle prods we sold them.

I would tell the audience that the real problem in Latin America wasn't the communists but the fact the people had no food, no land, and for some reason our government had the hardest time figuring that out.

"That may be," he would agree but he still felt we had to do something about those commies. We haven't talked much since Communism fell apart. I wonder if he has found something else that makes him feel strong.

"Do you want another Cuba?" he would always ask me. "Is that what you want?" This was his rationale for why we had to support every slimy government in South America.

"Are you actually lying awake at night worrying about Cuba?" I once asked him. "Are you worried about how they are going to show up tomorrow in Miami? What do you think they are going to do, swim all the way from Cuba holding their guns over their heads?"

"Of course not," he said. "Don't be silly, Gloria." Then what was he worried about?

I told him the only thing Castro had sent us in thirty years was his criminals and the lepers that came with boatpeople exodus in the '70s. Remember how ecstatic the Florida boat owners were? They were making a fortune, being paid to pick them up.

"Lepers," I shouted out to whomever else was listening. "We went and picked up their lepers like it was some blow for democracy."

But Cuba is finished, like Russia, so what does

Andrew worry about now? Probably nothing. People like Andrew don't worry about things.

I once asked Becky if she ever worried about something going wrong. I asked her if she worried about something happening to the kids or to their good life.

"Don't you ever worry that something bad is going to happen?" I asked her. She looked stunned at the question.

"No," she said. "Never."

A whole different breed.

*

As for the rest of the people who were there that day, this is all I know. Shotzy from Detroit was seen ten years ago in the New Orleans airport. She was still a stewardess on her way to someplace else. Andrew's Marjorie is alive and well and having late-life babies in Florida. O'Brien may have died in Viet Nam. Then again, he may be living in Wyoming.

Terry now weighs one hundred pounds less than he did in Mexico. He lives in New Jersey and is the vice president of a candy company. Terry is the one who told me what happened to Paul. About six or seven years ago he was in Memphis on business. He called out to that small town where Paul's mother used to live and Paul was still there. He was running the insurance business. His mother had died. Terry said he thought she died in some sort of accident but he didn't get all the details. I told him I hoped it was the one-armed black guy who finally got her.

He was the man she paid to clean the office and mow the lawn. He was an old veteran and he was broke. I never saw him but Paul told me about him. He said the man also had a drinking problem.

He laughed when he told me that his mother, that good Christian woman, paid the man two dollars for a few hours of cleaning the toilets, the garbage cans, washing the floors. He was laughing at the idea of a one-armed drunk trying to get it all done.

"She also threw in a six pack of beer if he did a real good job," he told me. Maybe that was true or maybe that was just Paul.

According to Terry, Paul was married and had one child, or two. I see him now as bald, a little stooped, bitter around the mouth. I don't think he was ever a happy man, at least not with me. Maybe there is some happiness now.

I haven't a clue about what happened to Ricardo's Cynthia. We always thought those two would get married. Ricardo did follow her to Buffalo but, as he told me that second trip to Mexico, he came back after a month.

"I couldn't live up there," he said. "Are you kidding? I saw the sun once in thirty days and then it was twelve degrees below zero. Even the weatherman on television was having some kind of breakdown because all he could forecast was more snow."

According to Ricardo, Buffalo was the worst place he had ever been and that was the last of Cynthia, a person who had not only lived there most of her life but who wanted to stay.

"She was difficult," he said. So was he with all that shouting about America and his endless cigarettes and the foot-in-the-mouth comment he made about my looks that second trip.

"You know, you look pretty good for your age," he told me. Apparently he had forgotten we were about the same age.

"So do you, jóven," I snapped back.

He knew the mistake he had made and he had been around enough American women to try and save himself.

"Ah, yes," he stammered, "I see what you mean, but you know how men are supposed to look good as they get older. For women it is different but, you know what I mean."

Oh, I knew what he meant and why he was dating a twenty-year-old model. I knew a lot about Ricardo that second trip down.

I had seen the rolled-up dollar bill wedged in the crook of the arm of the statue on his coffee table. I had seen the rolling papers in the kitchen drawer. I was there the night the model gave him a shot of vitamin B or something to ward off the hangover he knew he was due for the next morning. Ricardo was definitely a man of the '80s. I only hope that when he died under all the rubble he was drugged up and happy.

And me? I live with a drunk for a year before I know he drinks and then it is me who goes to the AA meeting filled with fear and guilt and self-loathing.

I still feel uncomfortable and almost frightened when people, men, women, even children,

ask me why I never married. I search for the right
words. I babble, smile, wave it all away and say I
could have been married a few times. That is almost true. I tell them the one I wanted to marry
wouldn't marry me. That is completely true. I tell
them I've loved men in my life and they, some of
them, have loved me. There was Baby James and
there was the Mexican.

He was there the first time and he loved me as
much as you can love anyone when you are nineteen or twenty. He was a nice man and had been
wining and dining me for weeks. Finally, he kissed
me. I could tell that kiss meant a lot to him but it
meant nothing to me. I wish it could have. What a
difference it would have made.

"You will see me again?" is what he asked me
but I could see that, just the like the doctor, the
lawyer, the married man, like Andrew, he already
knew the answer. This was only the last bit of hope
he had left.

"I am very busy," is what I told him. I was
moving into my American stage by then. But, oh,
how I wish that kiss had made a difference.

On that second trip to Mexico I actually tried
to find his number in the phone book but I wasn't
sure about his last name and Ricardo only vaguely
remembered him at all and cared even less. Eigh-
teen million people in that city and there I am
looking for his name in the phone book.

I would have liked to see him again. I still
would. He deserved the chance to treat me the way
I treated him that night but I would hope he
wouldn't. He was one of the decent ones.

So was Ricardo, in his way. I slept with him that first night back in Mexico City. He was one of my sixteen.

14

The end of the other story comes at the cars.

"We got back to our cars and then drove back to the city," Andrew tells them. I nod.

We don't tell them about the party afterwards which was the usual brawl. Joe and Becky had a fight. She threw his wallet and his keys out of the second story window and went home alone. Cynthia cut her hand playing with Paul's Swiss Army knife and Ricardo and some of others took her to the emergency room at the American hospital. O'Brien and some guys went on to Garibaldi Square and kept drinking. As usual, they got into some kind of trouble with the police but worked it out. Paul and I went to bed.

Maybe we didn't talk about the crucifixion that night. I don't think it was brought up again while we were down there but one year later I did get a copy of that newspaper article. I remind the listeners about the article.

"One of the guys down there sent it. The article said it never happened, that nobody was ever crucified in that little town."

Andrew and I smile at each other and chuckle. Then we stand. He moves to his visitor's side and we all go in to dinner. The story is finished.

*

I don't think I'll be telling the story again, not alone, not to shock someone or to make them think differently of me. I am not going to use it any more to entertain the troops. And I really don't think I will be telling it with Andrew. He is moving on to something else now. We haven't seen each other in almost two years and we haven't talked in months. Of course, he could surprise me, call me out of the blue, say he's in town and why don't we have dinner. That could happen but I don't think it will, not for a while, anyway.

I wonder what kept us in touch this long. All we have, after all, like Becky and Joe and I, is that year in Mexico, those parties, a few good times. Yes, and the crucifixion. But that has nothing to do with my life. That is only a story we tell.

I know a lot of people would say that something must have happened to me that day, to any of us who were there, that we must have been changed somehow or that it affected the rest of our lives. Americans love pointing to traumatic events, to crossroads, when you stopped drinking or cheating or when you found God. And if there was one life-changing moment, this certainly would have been it for me. But, it wasn't.

Nothing started for me that day and nothing ended. I wasn't religious before that day. I'm not religious now. I used to stop by a Catholic church every so often and go in and sit. Not for mass, but to sit alone. Sometimes I wanted the peace of an empty church but I haven't done that in years.

No, my life went on the way it was supposed to and my life hasn't been all that bad. I've made some mistakes and I've met a lot of people. I am healthy and the body is good for a few more years.

I still have a dream. I dream that someday I will buy a little truck with a camper. I will adopt a dog and travel around the country visiting the people I used to know. I will stay with them but spend the nights in my camper so I don't disrupt their lives too much. A little dream maybe, but that's all right.

Then the old reality snaps in. How long could I really do that? Two months, three, six? And where would I want to stop? There is nothing left to the old Phoenix. Dad's busy with his own life on Coronado. Hermosa Beach is awful now, filled with people and dirt. No more happy, slow, smiling people of the '70s, only naked butts flying around on roller blades.

I will never, and this is what counts, be young and pretty again. You have to be pretty to be forgiven all your sins, all your stupidities and lack of success. You're forgiven when you have potential, not when you're in your forties. What happened to me since that day is what happens to everybody. I got old.

I have had my sixteen men, one abortion, a psychiatrist for ten minutes and five cars. Only one of them was new and I totalled it after drinking too much at the Camelback Inn in Paradise Valley. Somebody else was buying, an Arab, I think, peach colored champagne. I had the accident right in front of a police car, rammed into an old Buick.

I thought I was going to jail. I cried for weeks until my hearing. I cried to my three-piece lawyer who laughed and told me, "People like you don't go to jail."

He was right, of course. I saw that the minute I walked into the courthouse. I wasn't going to jail in my clean little dress and low heels. They might be going, all the other people there with their t-shirts and dirty jeans, their hairy arm pits, those people putting out their cigarettes on the floor, but I wasn't. They sent me to a class instead.

Someone else told me the same thing, that things like that don't happen to people like me. Baby James. He asked me what I wanted to do, really wanted to do, and I said, go freelance, write a screenplay.

"What's stopping you?" he wanted to know. I told him I was scared of starving to death.

He laughed and said, "People like you don't starve." No, and we don't go to jail and maybe we don't write screenplays. We also don't buy new cars again. Another penance, I suppose, like the children I've never had.

I'm not going to have them now and I don't see men in my future, not when I'm being realistic. I've been celibate for the past two years, which used to be something of a religion in the '70s. Not for me, I am just not interested in anyone anymore.

I have had more than my fair share of sex and liquor and adventures so I suppose I can do without. Dad says, "You can't give up everything, Gloria." No, Dad, but I can try.

I used to have this dream of the future when I

would live in a house above the ocean, and there I am in this yellow and orange caftan flowing around me as I stand on the hill and watch my man as he pulls his small sailboat onto the beach with another man. There is no one, nothing around, but that sailboat and those two men standing knee deep in the water. Then a woman friend comes up to me, the other man is hers, and we put our arms around each other's waists and watch them below. We turn and move to the house, my house, with the ceiling-to-floor windows, wide open to the ocean and the sky. The white drapes are blowing out with the wind. Where is that house now?

I do fall in love, of course, and with the most unlikely men. I fall in love with the men I write about, one per project, artists, businessman. One was dead. I was doing a press kit for a Picasso exhibition. I studied everything about him, read everything. One day I realized he was in the room with me. I could see him, feel him scowling, assessing me for one of his fractured paintings. The old bastard. I fell in love with him and then smiled at him. Well, I have to love sometime, with whatever is offered.

I have been happy in my life although I don't know if it was really happiness or a kind of contentment. It only lasted a few minutes at a time. But again, my happiness or unhappiness has nothing to do with the crucifixion.

I didn't think about it for years. I never told anybody about it, not my father, not my sister, nobody. I never thought about it. If it had an impact, it would have had one on all of us, the ones who were there that day. What about Andrew and Becky and Joe and Terry? What about them? Those other people who were there that day went on and on and on, forever successful. Except for me.

Does any of that have to do with the crucifixion? Did we all reach that crossroads where decisions were made, lives changed irrevocably? Did some of us miss taking the right road while others, God's light in their eyes, moved forward on the path chosen at that moment when they saw the cross go up?

Nope. The only person whose life seems to change is that guy who gives up drinking, joins AA and goes to those nightly meetings which are as predictable as the pleasure he used to get from the first drink of the day. For one hour he revels in the horror of other people's stories. He laughs at the memory of how bad life was as a drinker and talks about how much his life has changed. Has it really? No. He is still dying for the thrill of the first drink of the night. And that's the end of that story.

The only impact that day may have had on me was that I can't look at crucifixes. If I am ever in a church, Catholic or otherwise, for a wedding or a funeral, I never look at the cross. In fact, I pray there isn't one. I may peek up to see if one is there, if it's bare, without the body hanging on it. But I don't want to see that either. I don't want to see them bare. I don't want to see them at all.

I don't remember if there was a crucifix in that church we ran to. There had to have been one, close to us, hanging right over us when we were sitting there but I don't remember it. It would have been one of those horrible, bloody Mexican ones. There had to have been one but I don't remember looking at it. I don't remember anyone looking at it. But I can remember how we were sitting in there, Andrew on one side of me, Paul on the other, the way we had been in that field. How could we not have seen that cross after what we had seen on the hill?

Lately I have been more and more aware of crosses. You see them everywhere here, church tops, billboards, behind some guy's head in an interview on television. But I've also caught myself seeing them in light patterns, shadows. I don't look for them but there they are.

My mother had a wonderful crucifix once. She bought it in Nogales, this large wooden cross with the head of Christ raised from it, all carved from one piece of wood. She hung it on the wall in her bedroom. Every once in a while she would say, "Did you ever notice how everyone makes Jesus look like them? In Africa he looks African, in Japan he looks Japanese. That Jesus is Mexican," she would say.

He was Mexican, right down to the long drooping mustache and the heavy lidded eyes and the full mouth. He was a passionate, sensuous-looking man, muy macho.

"Probably how he looked," Dad would say, "a strong man. He would have to be to carry that cross and to live through that part of it."

My mother loved the idea that people thought Christ looked like them. It pleased her, made her smile. That's the reason she bought the cross. I wonder what happened to it.

When Dad moved to California, a team of women came in and organized the garage sale. The cross could have gone then or could be in one of the boxes he kept of Mother's things. Someday I should ask him. I might want to have that cross. Like the old nun said, God will get you. But not yet. I did beg for time.

Maybe the screenplay will make a difference. It's not about the crucifixion. The man who said I should write about that day was wrong. I don't even like to talk about it. No, the screenplay is about women in advertising, a comedy in a way, a little sad too. It's about what we give up to get what we want and how it all works out in the end. Did for Becky and Joe and Andrew, didn't it?

I never did get to be an archeologist. I didn't find hidden treasures or old mummy men. I never even looked for them that first time in Mexico. On the other hand, I did see mountains that were pyramids. I sat on them. How many people have done that?

I still think about going back. I'd take the train this time. I might even want to ask Andrew if he wants to go or ask him if he'll meet me down there. I don't care who he is with now. We could have fun together. I could do that. I won't though.

*

I did forget something about that second trip to Mexico, about that dream I had of seeing some-one I knew, of having them run to me, hug me. I didn't see anyone those first days in the city but something happened when I got back to the city after those months in San Miguel.

I was in this cab going to the airport. We were on the Reforma, like in my dream. We were waiting at this stoplight when suddenly I saw someone I thought I knew. He was a guy who had come to Mexico to work on a dig in Oaxaca. He was from the south, from one of the Carolinas or Virginia. I leaned forward to get a better look at him. I was thinking about rolling down the window and yelling, "Marion, Marion, is that you?"

But the light changed and the cab moved ahead. All I could do was turn around and stare out the back window and watch as he crossed the street.

Why didn't I get out? Why didn't I stop the cab? And why, when we shot forward with the light, did I sit far back in the seat, hiding, so he couldn't see me as we passed?

Maybe it was all a dream. I am not sure now that I did see Marion or anyone who looked like him on that ride to the airport. Maybe I had dreamed of it happening so often that I now think it did.

Maybe I did almost adopt those children. Maybe I was there less than three months. Maybe I was the beautiful señorita with the red hair, the one the merchants all knew and loved. Maybe I did take the train back to the U.S. that second trip to prove I wasn't running away. Maybe we did stop at all the small towns and I walked outside at the stations, buying food from the vendors and learning that I was no longer young in Mexico.

So much of what happened or didn't happen

in Mexico has become part of my dreams. But I didn't dream the crucifixion. No sir. And I don't dream about it now.

Andrew

15

Gloria always could be a little intense, even for me, and I've known her for over twenty years. I like Gloria. One thing about her, she was never boring.

She and my father never got along. They got into it every time they were together. They would fight, usually about politics, and he would get to the point where he was so angry he was shouting at her. That's when she'd laugh and shake her head, the way she does. It used to drive him crazy. He'd yell at her, "Don't shake your head at me, young lady." Once he called her a bitch and she said she'd rather be a bitch than a Nazi. But by the end of the night they would be talking again and he would have calmed down. That's the way my father is. Once he gets something out of his system, he is fine.

My father is James Fritts. If you know contemporary Western art, you might know the name. He has been called the dean of Western artists. He has been painting the American Indian for more than forty years. He paints the Indians as they were before the white man came and then after we began to take over their land. His works are in a number of museums out here and he has collectors all over the country. The big East and West Coast critics don't like his kind of art but that doesn't bother him. He always says, "Who are they to say what art is? It ain't all Picasso."

He was supposed to be a lawyer, like his father, my grandfather, Walter Fritts. But art was always my father's first love. He left Dartmouth and moved to New York when he was only nineteen. His plan was to work and take classes during the day and paint at night, but the war broke out and he signed up like everyone else did back then. He spent the whole war in California drawing maps. He says to the Army drawing was drawing. When the war ended he went back to New York and went to City College on the GI Bill. That's where he met Mother. We were raised in Pound Ridge.

That was a great place to be a kid, very country, very safe, and it was an easy commute for my father. He was working for a book publisher in the city. He also did illustrations on the side for magazines like the *Saturday Evening Post* and *Colliers*. Many of the assignments were for art to go along with short stories about the old West, cowboys and Indians, shoot-outs, that sort of thing. He also got the covers quite a few times.

He had to do a lot of research and that's when he started getting interested in the American Indian. Every summer we would go out West for a few weeks. We'd stay in cabins or small hotels. He'd go to the reservations to paint and take pictures and we'd spend our time with Mother. There was usually a pool or lake nearby. It was great unless it rained, then we went crazy. There weren't televisions in every motel room back then.

Those vacations couldn't have been easy for

Mother. She still had to do all the cooking and the cleaning and the washing for three kids and she had to keep us entertained. But she never complained. And then, after he went free-lance, my father would take us out West for the whole summer.

We'd drive out there, stopping in Saginaw first to visit Grandfather. I never knew how he felt about Father's painting but he used to say to, "There were Indians here too, you know, Jimmy."

At the age of forty-two, younger than I am now, my father quit all the freelance work and decided to concentrate on his own art. That was quite a decision to make with three kids to support. He had absolutely no guarantee he would be able to make a living; few artists ever have. He had been able to sell a few of his Indian paintings at local galleries so he knew there was some interest. Still, it took a lot of courage to make a career change at that age. I don't think I could have done it.

The year I went to Dartmouth, they sold the house in Pound Ridge and moved to Evergreen, Colorado. My sister Christina was already on her own, trying to build a modeling career in New York. My younger brother Billy made the move with them. The move made sense. They could get a cheaper place out there and my father was closer to his subject and to people who really liked his work. They stayed in Colorado fifteen years, then moved to Sedona, Arizona where they've been ever since.

"I would have been a miserable lawyer," Father always says. He's right. He would have been a terrible lawyer. He is far too opinionated and too willing to let his opinion be known by everyone, no matter how insulting it might be. He would be destroyed in a court of law. Worse than that, his client would be. He has none of the subtleties you need to win a jury or a judge.

He can be a difficult man to like if you don't know him well. He is very German in his belief in his importance as the father of the house. The house is his house, the rules are his rules, his needs are to be met first, and then everything will be calm. One of the rules we had as kids was that we all had to sit down together every night for dinner as a family, regardless of any other activities we had planned, sports, dates. We would complain to Mother but she'd only say, "That's what your father wants."

But Father wasn't that bad. Sometimes he would laugh at himself for being so stiff-necked about things. There was the one night when we all must have had someplace else to go. We were sitting at the dining room table eating as fast as we could, shoveling the food in. No one was saying anything, just rushing to get through the meal so we could leave. Finally, there was this deep silence and we all looked up at the same time. There was Father sitting at the head of the table glaring at us.

He shouted, "Where in the name of God is the fire?" We all burst out laughing, all the food we had crammed into our mouth, potatoes, milk, flying out. He was laughing too and then told us to get the hell out and go where we had to go.

We had a lot of good times. The summers we spent out West were fun and there were two summers when we went to Mexico. We stayed in the town of San Miguel de Allende. San Miguel was one of the old silver cities during the colonial period. Then it became a kind of mecca for American artists. Still is, as far as I know. My father was down there taking classes at the Institute and we stayed in a hotel that had a swimming pool. We'd spend every morning in the pool and in the afternoons Mother would take us sightseeing or shopping. Sometimes we'd take the bus over to Guanajuato. That's where Christina and I always wanted to go because of the mummies.

There was a graveyard there with hundreds of mummies. Mother couldn't have had any idea of what she was getting us into when she took us there. She probably thought it was some kind of museum. We never went back no matter how much Christina and I used to beg her to take us to see the mummies.

Christina and I used to search through all the little stores for post cards of the mummies to scare Billy. We would hide them under his pillow or put them on his plate before he came down to breakfast. He was still a little kid and he was terrified of the mummies. We were always telling him we were going to take him back to the graveyard. It made Mother furious because it got to the point where it was almost impossible to get him on a bus to go anywhere. He'd be kicking and screaming and all the Mexican mothers would be looking at Mother and she'd say. "It's not me. It's not me." Christina and I would get in the back of the bus and laugh all the way to Guanajuato. Poor Billy. He was such a good kid, and those mummies were gruesome.

As I understand it, the family graves were dug straight down, not across like we do in this country. The bodies were placed on top of one another and when the grave was full or if the family couldn't pay anymore, the skeletons were taken out and put in a shed, a charnel house. But apparently in this particular graveyard there is something in the soil that preserves some of the bodies and some of them were put on display. You could see mummy mothers holding mummy babies, old people, children, and some of them looked like they were screaming, like they had been buried alive. Poor Mother, she got us out of there fast.

I don't know if the families of these people okayed putting their family members on display. If it had to do with not paying their bills, I suppose they didn't have much of a choice. Also, I think these were very old mummies. Maybe nobody even knew who they were. But they sure were the high point of those trips to Mexico for me and Christina.

My father doesn't do that kind of traveling anymore. He doesn't have to. He is close enough to the Navajo and Hopi reservations to drive up there and back in a day if he needs to but he does most of his work at home now. He has quite a collection of Indian artifacts, tomahawks, headdresses, clothes, blankets. He also has a library of books on the American Indian. He is known for his authenticity. If there is a blanket on the back of an Indian pony in a James Fritts painting, you know it would be the exact blanket that would have been on the back of that particular horse on that day. The critics and writers about Western art always mention how detail-oriented my father is.

He is not dumb about art. He studied art for years. He still does. He can recognize genius in the most avant-garde work. He thought Marjorie had talent and told her so. He said he liked what she was doing and she always thought her art was way out there. But, overall, his feeling about modern art is that it has no more validity than any other type of art well done. It's a difficult opinion to argue even if you disagree.

My father always worked hard. When we were growing up he would spend a full day working in New York and then come home and paint in his studio until after midnight. He painted every day of his life, including holidays. I can't remember one time when he sat down and watched a football game from beginning to end. He was always in his studio either painting or reading.

Mother used to handle the business end of his work. She was the one who did the phone calling, wrote the letters. She was the one who went to the galleries and kept in touch with the people who liked his art. She let them know about the new pieces he was working on in case they might be interested in buying. I know it must have been hard for her because Mother is really very shy but every artist needs that kind of support. Artists usually aren't good about business or about people, for that matter. My father's success had a lot to do with Mother. My ex-wife Barbara used to say, "I wish I had a wife like your mother."

Now my father's art business is handled by a

Scottsdale gallery and another one in Jackson Hole. He does have to go out and meet the public, to press the flesh, so to speak. He has to be there for the openings and the museum shows. They also do some entertaining at home. Collectors go up to Sedona to see what he is working on. It is certainly worth his time to see them since his paintings now go for well over a hundred thousand dollars, an incredible figure for a living artist.

He says it is because they are all betting on him dying soon. "The vultures are coming," he always says whenever collectors are on their way up to the house.

Barbara used to say they'd be sorry, that he would outlive us all out of pure spite. She never got along with him, although she did try. I know that. What Barbara never understood was that you don't argue with my father. He is always going to win. The family knows this. We let him go on and on about whatever it is that is bothering him. Then he's finished and everything goes back to normal. But Barbara would never let something go. She thought when he brought something up it was open for discussion and possible disagreement.

I have to say in her defense that my father was even more difficult when it came to her. Barbara couldn't say anything around him without starting him off. We would be up at the house and Mother would ask her what she would like to eat or drink and if she asked for something that they didn't have, my father would hit the roof. He took this as a personal criticism, as though she had spent the entire trip from California planning what she could ask for that he wouldn't have in the house.

She couldn't win no matter what she did. If she said she didn't want anything in particular, that anything would be okay, that would get him angry. He'd say, "You must have some idea of what you want, something." Luckily, Barbara drank a lot of water.

She still calls him The Duke, for John Wayne, someone else she never liked. She always said she had the feeling John Wayne didn't like women, even with all of his old world charm. She felt the same way about my father.

She started with the Duke business when my father started wearing the boots and the cowboy hat. Barbara thought it was silly but it has to do with the group he belongs to, the Artists of the American West. They all paint or sculpt themes of the old West. There are no trucks or cars in their paintings. There are fifteen active members, all men, another thing Barbara went on and on about. But, in Western art circles, it is considered quite an honor to be a member.

One of the things they do is wear cowboy boots and hats and western-cut suits at their annual shows in Santa Fe. It's like a group signature. Barbara thought it was ridiculous since most of the artists weren't from the West. Most of them were like my father. They were raised in the Midwest or the East and came from a commercial art background. But there are also artists in the group who were raised in the West, who were real cowboys.

My father used to say that the whole Western look, the hat and the boots, made him feel like an idiot but that it helped sell paintings. Now I think he likes it and what's the harm? He does have a bit of John Wayne about him. He's tall, thin. He looks good for a man his age and the boots and hat look good on him. They're not something I'd wear but then I don't live where he does. It works in Sedona and they love it in Europe. In France they call him Le Cowboy, which is what I believe they used to call Reagan. They like his work over there, especially in Germany and France. The Japanese are also buying Western art.

He was a good father. He never raised his hand to any of us, and I know he cared about us. He is a good man. You only have to know when to let things drop with him. Barbara never did learn that. She said it was ridiculous to let him go on and on about something and not tell him when he was wrong or out of line.

She was always saying, "Why do you let him say things like that? Why don't you say something?" I knew better. Finally, she stopped holding back. She would tell him when he was wrong. She'd tell him if he said something mean to someone. She wouldn't let anything pass.

She used to say, "What do I have to lose? He never liked me anyway." I told her she was wrong, that if she would just accept him the way he was, if she wouldn't argue with him, everything would be fine. She said it wouldn't make any difference what she did because he didn't like her.

She was right. After we broke up he told me he had never liked her, not from the very beginning, that he always knew I would have trouble with her.

He said she was too demanding and that all she ever wanted was a way out of Chicago and a house in Burlingame. Well, that's what she got.

She was wrong, though, about his not liking women. He does like women. He's liked the women I've dated since our divorce, the ones he's met. He liked Karen a lot. He said, "You better keep this one, Andrew." I didn't but that wasn't my fault and it did work out for the best.

Gloria was something else. We never dated but she would come up to Sedona whenever I was there and they would go at it like cats and dogs. She is very liberal in her politics and my father is very conservative. "Andrew's little hippy," is what he called her. Gloria was never a hippy, carefree, yes, but not a hippy. She is, without a doubt, the most interesting woman I've ever known.

I met her the year I lived in Mexico. She was with Paul Monroe then but I had a terrible crush on her. I've told her that but she acts like she doesn't believe me. Once she said, "Why didn't you tell me then?" I always thought she knew. I was always over at the apartment even when Paul wasn't there. We used to go to the English movies together or we'd sit around talking for hours. I got to know her pretty well.

I had a great time, that year in Mexico. I liked the country and I liked the people. I met some good people down there. There was this one family who lived upstairs from me. On New Year's Eve the son came down and asked me if I wanted to come upstairs to their party. I took Gloria up there. Paul was still in the Yucatan with some of the guys.

Gloria had this bottle of champagne with her that she brought back from Arizona to share with Paul. I'll never forget that bottle. It was Laurent-Perrier. You never see it anywhere except in the best liquor stores. It must have cost her a fortune.

The family upstairs was middle class by Mexican standards but relatively poor by ours. There were four or five of them living in an apartment smaller than mine. They had pushed all the furniture against the walls and everyone was sitting around the edges of the room talking. They had this old record player. Couples would get up and dance or the children would. The Mexicans were so big on children. Really loved them.

They kept passing me a bottle of tequila. Gloria was drinking something else, probably rum and coke, but I was taking straight shots from the bottle. I remember everything about that night.

I was sitting in a big chair and Gloria was sitting at my feet. I was playing with her hair. She had this long, thick, dark reddish hair. I was playing with it and sort of patting her on the head. Boy, was I happy. I wasn't even getting drunk on the tequila. All I wanted to do was spend the night with her and drink that bottle of champagne. I wasn't thinking about how Paul would feel. I wasn't thinking about anything. I was completely happy. I think it was probably one of the best nights of my life. When I think about it now I get the same kind of feeling, content but sort of excited, like something great was going to happen. Everything was perfect.

I never went back to Mexico City. Friends of

mine who have been down there tell me how horrible it is. They say the smog is out of control and it
can take an hour to drive one mile on the Reforma.
They say parts of the city look like a war zone
because they still haven't cleaned up from the earthquake back in '85. I don't want to see the city like
that.

Mexico City was a fantastic place when I was
there and I had a great year, met good people.
There was only one bad time for me down there
and that was the day we saw the man die. That was
one of the worst days of my life, really. But, then,
that was only one bad day out of a whole great
year.

16

Law skipped a generation in my family. I became the lawyer. Our firm is not the biggest nor even the best in Los Angeles but we have a good client base and I am a full partner. My field is tax law; specifically, business investment tax law; more specifically, real estate investment and development tax law. The interesting element in this field is the constant changes and reinterpretation of the tax code. You have to stay on top of it. It's not my grandfather's kind of law but I enjoy it.

Grandfather was a wonderful man. He practiced law all of his life in Saginaw, Michigan. He loved the law more than anything in life. He used to tell me, and these are his exact words, "There is nothing as great, as important, as worthy of study and commitment as the law." He would bellow that out in that loud voice of his. He said the body of Western law was a living work of art.

He was a tall man, over six-two, with a head of thick white hair which he had until the day he died. His hair turned white in his twenties. He said it happened overnight. When I was young he told me it happened after he heard how the government joined the coal mine owners in shooting striking miners. He said he was so furious that when he woke up the next morning his hair was white. Knowing Grandfather and his political beliefs, it is possible. No one else in this family ever turned white young.

Grandfather died at ninety-eight in his own bed. His heart finally gave out. His mind wandered a little in those last years but the few times I was able to get up to see him he would have long periods when he was right on the money. He said to me once, "Did you ever think I'd get so old, Andy?" That's what he called me, Andy. Nobody else ever did.

One time he asked me how old he was. He waited until Aunt Christina left the room. I told him he was ninety-four or five, however old he was then. His eyes got big and he yelled at me, "There is no way in hell I am ninety-four" or whatever age it was.

I told him it was true and he gave me that look of his, where he would tilt his head to one side and narrow his eyes as though judging the truth of what you were saying. Then he said, "Well, what the hell do you know, Jimmy?" He thought I was my father. He also told me not to tell Aunt Christina how old he was. He said she was already treating him like an old fool.

I have his desk at home in my office. It's so big it barely fits in there but I don't care. That's where I want it. My girlfriend Maureen has been helping me with some decorating and she says she's going to leave my office alone because it should be whatever I want it to be. She likes the desk too. It's one of those old ones with the leather top and gold leaf inlay around the edges. The wood is very dark and very heavy. I also have the old wooden swivel chair he used to use.

The desk wouldn't work at all in my office in the city. Not because of the size, I have a large office, but because we try to keep the look very light, clean. Not a high tech look per se but very professional and modern, the look we want to present to our clients. Grandfather's desk is a little old-world for our office.

Grandfather's office in Saginaw was very different from mine. The walls were dark, lined with books. There were big leather easy chairs. I clearly remember a spittoon by the corner of his desk. My father says that's impossible, that he never had a spittoon anywhere in his office, but I remember one being there.

The whole family was always a little afraid of Grandfather. He had four children and they would all jump to attention whenever he came into a room, including my father. Grandfather would sit in his rocking chair next to the big console radio and he would give me chocolate kisses from a bag he kept hidden behind the cabinet. I wasn't afraid of him at all and when he wasn't around I would go into that room and sneak the candy.

He was the kind of lawyer who could handle all types of cases. You could do that back then. It's different now. Now you have to specialize, like all the professions.

Grandfather liked criminal law the best, I believe. That's when he could do it up right. He could march around the courtroom and play up to the jury. He must have been good at that with that big booming voice of his, but I never saw him in action.

By the time I was a kid he was semi-retired and we only got over to Saginaw once or twice a year. I do know he had an incredible acquittal record, something like ninety percent. If Grandfather defended you, you got off.

"They weren't all innocent, you know." That's what my father once told me about the people Grandfather defended. I couldn't have been more than eight or nine when he told me that and I'm not sure I needed to hear that then. But, of course, they couldn't all have been innocent, could they?

I never have to go into a courtroom, and that's fine by me. I know I wouldn't do well in that kind of law. My work is on paper. It probably would seem pretty dull to Grandfather but I enjoy it. We don't try to affect major changes through law. We represent our clients the best we can. For me and the lawyers I work with, the law is a tool. For Grandfather it was a philosophy of life.

His family came to this country from Germany in the 1800s and settled in the Midwest. They were Fritzes then, not Fritts. The name was changed to make it read more American. I don't know exactly why they came because, as I understand it, they were always professional people in Germany. It may have been because of war or looking for new opportunities.

Education has always been important in our family. Grandfather prepped at Andover, so did my father. I went to Choate but only for one year. All of us went to Dartmouth but only Grandfather graduated from there. My father made it through the first year then packed it up and went to New

York. I didn't even make it that far. I had to leave my first year because of my grades. It is possible that we both disappointed Grandfather badly but he never said a word, not to me at least.

He had been taking me to Dartmouth every chance he got. He would stop by Pound Ridge to pick me up for a big game or a reunion. Sometimes we would go up there for the weekend just to pal around. He would introduce me to everyone he knew on campus and to everyone he thought I should know, not because they were important but because he thought they were interesting. We talked to the professors, the librarians, the cooks. There was a janitor up there who knew everyone and everything they had done right and wrong as students. I loved that school. I wanted more than anything else to go there. That was my dream.

Grandfather always said he had spent the best years of his life at Dartmouth. I can remember how he used to march across that campus talking about the things he had done there and pointing out different buildings. When I was a kid I would have a hard time keeping up and he would stop and say, "Aren't you in this game, Fritts?"

But it didn't work out. I never was a great student, good but not great. Even as a legacy, I needed that extra year at Choate before Dartmouth would accept me. That was after I graduated from public high school. Maybe if I had been in private schools from the beginning, it would have made a difference but my father didn't want his children in private schools. He said the schools in Westchester County were as good as any prep school. And besides, he was paying for them in his taxes. That's what he said. Money might have been a problem. There were three of us. But money was never discussed in our home. I would say we were always comfortable even when he was freelancing. There was also money on Mother's side.

The year at Choate didn't help. I did miserably at Dartmouth. I barely made it through any classes. I had never learned how to knuckle down and study and I was doing a lot of partying with the other guys. By spring, the suggestion was made that I might take a little time off, maybe go to another school in the fall. They said they might consider readmitting me but I was going to have to prove myself somewhere else first.

I was devastated even though I knew it had to happen. I couldn't tell Grandfather. I think Mother did that. When I tried to talk to him later, he sort of waved me off. He said, "I know you'll work it out, Andy." I promised myself I would make it up to him somehow.

For most guys my age it would have been a terrible time to be out of college and not married. Viet Nam was going strong and everybody was going in. With that extra year at Choate I was almost twenty and just what the Army wanted. But it turned out I was a solid 4-F. When I was seven I slipped on some ice in the driveway and broke my right leg. It never bothered me, still doesn't, but that leg is almost an inch shorter than my left one. That was enough to keep me out.

I went out to Colorado to stay with my parents and got the toughest job I ever had in my life.

I worked construction doing roofs. Miserable work. Ten, fifteen hours a day. If it wasn't hot, it was raining and cold. It was enough to make me want to get back to college fast. That's where I met Frank Coppola. Construction was his summer job. He was going back to school in Mexico in the fall, the American college down there and he said I might want to come along with him. At that point it sounded like a good idea. I had the money. I had the money I made in construction and there was also a trust fund that had been set up for me by Granny McCabe, Mother's mother, to pay for school.

Besides, I wasn't ready for another heavy duty college. I knew some school in Mexico would never get me back into Dartmouth but I would have something to do until I figured out what I really wanted to do next. And I liked Mexico from those summers I spent down there. Frank said there were a lot of schools in Mexico City that catered to Americans, language schools where I could study Spanish. So I went back with him in September.

There were at least ten million people living in Mexico City then but it was like a small town. All of the Americans down there knew each other, the students, the guys and gals who had been born down there, whose parents worked for the American companies. We all knew each other. We went to the same parties, played touch football on Sundays in Chapultepec Park. It was great.

I met Paul Monroe and Joe Pajorski right off the bat. They had an apartment off Melchor Ocampo. Terry Seiffert was a friend of theirs. He was this heavy-set guy from Fort Lewis, New Jersey. Joe was from Gary, Indiana. He was the son of a first generation Polish factory foreman. Joe was small but very solid. He used to play high school football. He said he wasn't big enough for college ball. I think that may have bothered him.

He was dating Becky Palmer, Becks, a very pretty blond from Dallas who was staying with friends down there and taking art classes or something like that. Her father owned a trucking company. She ended up with Joe and they might have seemed like an unusual couple. She was wealthy and elegant in that flashy Texas kind of way and Joe was pretty basic, but they were both from blue collar backgrounds. Her father had just made a lot of money. Probably a very smart man.

Paul Monroe was an interesting guy. He was good-looking, blond, six feet or six-one. The girls loved him. They fell over him. He had that Paul Newman kind of look, the square jaw, good smile, but his eyes weren't that sky blue like Newman's. They were dark. He wasn't as good-looking as Newman, but close.

He always had a deal going. He came back to Mexico that year with a trunk full of American underwear. He was selling shorts to the Mexicans for an incredible profit but they sold so fast he had to start selling his own. Then he sold Joe's. And when they both ran out he started offering anyone who came to the apartment cash for their shorts. He'd say, "Take 'em off now, I'll pay ya."

Of course, you weren't going to get anything like what he was charging the Mexicans but some of the guys were down to their last pair of shorts before he closed up shop. He was something else.

We were all slightly perverted then but nobody could beat Paul. He had drilled holes all over their apartment. Whenever they had a party, all the guys would go into his bedroom and look through the hole into the bathroom when one of the girls was in there. I know it sounds awful now but I only went in there once or twice. You couldn't see anything but Paul would get so excited about some girl going into the bathroom that it was funny. Most of the time we would just be laughing at how excited he got. That didn't last long. Becks, or maybe it was Gloria, put her foot down and made Joe plaster up the holes.

Then there was the time Paul really lucked out. A young newlywed couple moved in across the street. He said they had to be newlyweds because they were going at it all the time. He knew that because you could see right into their bedroom by standing up on the roof. They had the blinds turned the wrong way. That was all Paul needed. He told everybody there was a show going on and to come over to the apartment.

It was true. The guy would come home every afternoon and head straight for the bedroom and then they would go at it. After a few days there must have been ten guys up on Paul's roof watching. It got so bad Paul was telling Gloria to make them popcorn. I went up once but that was all. The girl was beautiful. She had this beautiful figure, long legs. She didn't look Mexican except for the long dark hair.

It isn't something I'm proud of or something

I would ever do again but it wasn't mean-spirited for any of us. It was something guys do at that age. Except for that one time, I stayed downstairs and talked to Gloria.

Then all of a sudden it stopped. The guy wasn't coming home in the afternoon and when he finally did, nothing happened. They never went into the bedroom. Paul went crazy. He figured they had a fight and he kept waiting for them to make up. The rest of us didn't care. We did what we usually did, stayed downstairs drinking beer and playing cards, but Paul spent all of his time on the roof waiting and working on ways of getting them back together.

Finally, he and Ricardo, this Mexican guy we knew, went to the flower market and bought about fifty roses. They paid a boy to take them to the wife and told him not to tell her where they came from. They wanted her to think they were from her husband. Gloria said it was a bad idea, that the guy might end up in a fight with the wife, thinking they came from somebody else but that didn't stop Paul.

We all watched the flowers being delivered from the living room window, then we went up on the roof, including some of the girls. We had all been listening to Paul go on and on about this for at least a week and we wanted to see what would happen.

Sure enough, the guy comes home and they both head for the bedroom. You can imagine Paul. He was laughing and cheering. It was going to work. But then, before anything happens, the man walks to the window, looks out for a long time and then shuts the blinds completely. Paul said he must have spotted us up on the roof, and there was a line of people up there by then, but what I think happened was that he realized that if he could see out then somebody else could see in.

Paul was furious. He couldn't believe it. He was up there shouting and moaning for the guy to open the blinds. We were all laughing so hard we were on the ground. All of his plans, all that money for roses, and the man had shut the blinds. We loved it.

For weeks Paul moaned about those blinds. He would look out the window and start shouting about them. He worked on plans to get them open again. At one point he and Ricardo were actually planning to go in disguised as repairmen when the husband was at work. He also worked on an idea to buy the wife drapes and say they came from the landlord. Anything to get those blinds down. But it didn't happen. As far as I knew, they never opened them again and you can bet he kept checking.

You had to like the guy. He was always up for something. He could make you laugh with his schemes. Nothing ever worked the way he thought it would. That was what was so funny about Paul. The only thing I didn't like about him was the way he treated Gloria. He would give her orders, criticize her clothes, her cooking, the way she looked, everything, but she would only laugh. I wouldn't call it abusive and it didn't seem to bother her, but I didn't understand why she put up with it. Why didn't she say something to him, tell him to shut up?

I was dating Marjorie by then. We met the first month I was there. She was studying art at the National University and we ended up staying together for almost three years. We left Mexico together and went up to Chicago. She went to the Art Institute and I went to the University of Chicago. It had a good reputation, still does. I still think one of the reasons I was accepted was that they thought I was a foreign student since all of my paperwork had come from Mexico.

Chicago was a good town and I didn't want to go back East. I didn't want to be anywhere near Dartmouth unless I was going there. I never did apply for readmission. By then I was already two years older than my class and I really didn't think I would be able to get back in. I didn't want to face that. I graduated from the University of Chicago and went on to law school there. I passed the Illinois bar the second time around. It was tough.

I know my going into law made Grandfather happy and I have no complaints about it. I have a good life and I think I'm a good lawyer. I make a good living, even after taxes, just like my grandfather and my father.

17

Thinking about Gloria and those Mexico days makes me laugh. For some reason she pretends she didn't know how much I liked her. She also claims she doesn't remember what happened that night, that New Year's Eve. I've asked her if she remembers but she says no and changes the subject. We got into it that night. We went back to my apartment and it got pretty hot and heavy for a while but nothing really happened. Maybe it's just as well. I may have one of those guy fantasies every once in a while about going off with her for a few days, doing nothing but eating oysters, drinking champagne and making love, but I know there could never have been anything more between us.

For one thing, everything about Gloria was always on the edge. She was always moving or changing jobs or talking about it. She never had any kind of plan for a future. Nothing was ever long-range with her. Always spur of the moment. It would be hard to live with that twenty-four hours a day. You want to know what somebody is going to do next. You need to. You reach a point in life where you want things calm and steady. That's not Gloria.

My ex-wife used to call her my cowgirl. The first time she met her she acted surprised. She said, "That's Gloria?" as though she was expecting something completely different. I don't know what she was expecting. I told her what Gloria was like but Barbara always was a bit of a Vassar snob. Gloria was probably wearing those tight jeans and boots she always wore. Barbara said she looked a little "country." I find that funny now coming from a woman who ran off with a guy who wore nothing but shorts and hiking boots. I guess that wasn't too country for her.

It still hurts, the whole thing. It never made any sense to me. I thought she was going through some kind of phase, that eventually it would be over and done with and we could get back to normal. I was willing to overlook what had happened, to go into counseling, anything she wanted to keep the marriage together, but that wasn't what she wanted. I come home one night and she tells me either I have to leave or she is going to take Ashley and go to a hotel. It was crazy. It came right out of the blue. I thought we had a good marriage, a happy marriage. I know I was happy and she never complained, not about anything big.

She said it had nothing to do with Dan Green. Now that I don't believe. I never liked the guy. He had been coming over to the house to work with her on some kind of marketing project for one of her classes. That's what I thought. By my estimation, they had been having an affair for at least a month before she told me she wanted a divorce. She says that's not the case, that they were friends until the separation. I didn't believe it then and I don't believe it now. The reasons she gave for wanting a divorce didn't make sense, not unless he was involved.

She said she wasn't happy and hadn't been happy for a long time. Could have fooled me. She wouldn't even discuss it because she said she didn't want to hurt my feelings by saying anything more and I shouldn't push it. Here I am standing in my own living room and she's telling me I shouldn't ask her why she wants a divorce.

I never in my life thought I would be a divorced man. In my family you married for life. That's the way I went into it. You didn't go into marriage thinking you could always get a divorce, the way people do now. I know she had to have been having an affair with Green and I don't know why she won't admit to it. It certainly doesn't matter now.

I didn't think of him as any kind of threat. I didn't think he was the kind of guy she would be interested in. He managed a small camping supply store in Burlingame. He was into all of that, camping, hiking, river-running. Barbara never cared about things like that. She was into the house and decorating and gardening. As far as I knew, she had never been camping or hiking in her life. Now she goes all the time. Green wasn't a good-looking guy and he wasn't making much money back then. What was the attraction? I don't know.

When I met Barbara she was a Vassar grad working in Marshall Field's. She didn't know what she wanted to do with her life. I was in law school. Marjorie and I had split up the year before. The '70s were like that. People lived together for a while, then split. Back then people our age weren't supposed to have serious relationships, not ones that ended in marriage. Everybody was supposed to be free to do their own thing, that was the expression, do your own thing.

Marjorie's thing was her art and she said she needed to be in New York to do it. At that point, she was doing collages on canvas, very experimental, she thought. She said she couldn't grow as an artist in Chicago. She needed to be around real artists. She didn't like the Midwest. She said it was constricting. She said, "I need to be where art is happening."

I argued with her about it. I said, Chicago, New York, it didn't matter. You did your art wherever you were and if she couldn't be an artist in Chicago then she probably couldn't be an artist anywhere else. Besides, I thought we were happy together. I had no problems at all with the relationship. Looking back, I know I wasn't in love with her but things were working out and I wanted to stay together. Things were great. I was graduating. I had been accepted in law school. She was doing some teaching. But it was the '70s and everybody was supposed to be free. She left and went to New York to find herself. That was another expression. Man, I've got to find myself.

The funny thing is she didn't stay there that long. She met some guy and they got married and moved to Florida. She has two kids, teenagers now. We stay in touch. I get a Christmas card from her every year. On the back it says M.M. Larimore Designs. That's her name, Marjorie May Larimore, so apparently she never took her husband's name,

Williamson, Jack Williamson. He has a print shop in Tampa where they must do the cards.

She usually sends a newsletter and a photo with the card. I noticed this year how much older she looks. She is much heavier now and is wearing her hair short. She doesn't dress that arty way she always did. The husband looks okay, about my age.

Overall, I don't think I've changed that much since my twenties. I try to keep in shape, eat right. I started playing tennis a few years ago and I have a membership at the racquet club where I can work out a few days a week. Maybe I am losing some hair, but who isn't. Of course, there have been the changes that come with maturity. I don't drink much anymore, certainly not the way I did back in Mexico. There were times down there when I can remember waking up still drunk after some party. Then we'd head out for 'pulco or the Yucatan. No plans, not much money, but off we'd go. You can't do that kind of thing now, not at any age, not in Mexico.

I never thought about how dangerous it was traveling down there twenty years ago. We were driving back and forth to the border, taking trains down to Vera Cruz. The girls did it too. Becks used to take the train all the way from Texas to Mexico City by herself. Can you imagine an American mother allowing that today? I can't. I wouldn't let Maureen do it. It's too dangerous down there. It always was. What was Becks' mother thinking of?

Those girls did everything. We used to go to the whorehouses in Acapulco and they'd come too.

I was surprised the first time that happened but Joe said they didn't care. They were like our sisters. They would hold our wallets when we danced with the girls.

The first time I went I hadn't started dating Marjorie. The guys egged me on and I paid for a girl who couldn't have been more than fifteen or sixteen. They were all young, the pretty ones, and we didn't think about their ages then. We were young too. I was only twenty. I gave her a couple of hundred pesos and she almost cried. That was a lot of money for her and for me. She was a pretty little thing, long black hair, very much an Indian. I never saw her again when we went back there, but by then I was with Marjorie and she came with us like the rest of the girls.

The name of the place was the Burro, El Burro. The guys told me there was a woman there who did it with a burro, like a floor show. I never saw that but I did see a burro tied to a palm tree outside so maybe it was true. It was an incredible place, like a giant thatched hut, all open, except for the rooms where you went with the girls.

I know it sounds sordid but it wasn't that way. It was fun. Nobody got hurt. It was a different time. I admit I sometimes miss it, the way it was down there, the way I was in Mexico. We were all so free. We did whatever we wanted, no plans, no worries. You felt like your whole life was in front of you and it was.

I miss the guys down there. I have good male friends now but we are all involved with our own lives. You know, you have friends at work and friends for tennis. Down there we were all connected. People were always running in and out of each other's apartments. You never were alone. Something was always going on. You couldn't even walk down the street without seeing someone you knew. Eleven million people and you always saw someone you knew. Where else could that happen? That doesn't happen to me in LA.

I wasn't bored for one minute in Mexico, not that I am bored now. I like my life but it is different when you are an adult. You can't be free the way you were when you were nineteen or twenty years old. You have responsibilities but that doesn't mean you're bored. And it doesn't mean you are a boring person.

Marjorie once told me I was boring. She said I wasn't into doing exciting things, that I didn't know how to live life. This is when I am trying to make the grades to get into law school. How exciting could I be? I wonder how exciting the printer is. How exciting is it to design the family Christmas card?

Barbara was another one. She used to say her life was boring, meaning our life was boring. That's why she said she wanted to go back to school. I said fine but I wasn't bored with our life. I loved our life. I had a good job. I was supporting a family. That's not boring. Now Barbara is running her own business and trying to stay afloat and raise a child. Is that exciting enough for her? Pretty tough, I'd say. But that's what she wanted.

She's become quite the businesswoman. She is always being quoted in magazines and newspapers out here. She talks about how mothers can combine careers with raising a child. There was even a spot on a national television show where she was talking about her child-raising theories. I find that interesting. She was only home a few months with Ashley before she decided she wanted to go back to school. So even as a baby, Ashley was in day care part of the time. Now Barbara has a full-time housekeeper. I'm not saying Barbara is a bad mother, she loves Ashley. But whatever the articles say, Barbara has spent most of Ashley's life either in school or running a business. I didn't know that was what she wanted.

Now she's living in the city with Allen Renkin. He quit his marketing job to work with her. Barbara's company has really taken off. She started designing and selling toys for advanced children a few years ago. I think part of her success is due to her selling herself so well, all those articles. She says it is because every parent thinks her child is advanced, so they buy the toys. She was recently listed as one of the leading start-up small business people of the year by *Money Magazine*.

She and Allen do a lot of traveling and now she says she is going to write a book about traveling with children. She says she is going to sell it herself through her catalog. And guess who is going to carry her book in his catalogs? Good old Dan Green. Now he's got his own mail order business. I see his ads in airline magazines. He also organizes outdoor trips. She stayed with him for about a year after the divorce. He actually moved into the house. That really bothered me. That's probably what got me to make the move to LA. I couldn't stand the thought of that bastard being in my house.

I think my father was more upset about the house than about the divorce. He is always telling me how that house was legally mine, that I bought and paid for it and I was wrong to let Barbara have it. But I did. I let her have the house because I wanted Ashley to be raised there, to stay in that neighborhood. I never thought twice about giving her the house, and they did stay there until she sold it last year. Now she says she and Allen are going to buy a townhouse together in the city.

That was hard, when she sold the house. I really loved that house. We had some good times there. I could have worked it so I maintained half ownership, so she couldn't sell it, or not as easily, but I didn't want that. I didn't want a mean divorce. My father could never understand that.

We found the house right after we moved to California. The law firm I went with in Chicago had been representing a major client with growing real estate interests out here. They offered me a job as their in-house counsel, working out of their San Francisco office. It was a good move for us. Barbara's buying job at Marshall Field's wasn't what she should have been doing. I told her that often enough. She was too smart for that. At first she thought we should live in the city but after we found the house she realized Burlingame would be a great place to live and it was an easy commute for me.

Everything was perfect. I liked corporate law.

Barbara got a buying job in the city and we bought the house. We were very happy together, always working on the house, fixing it up.

When we bought it there was no lawn to speak of, no garden. The house hadn't been painted in years, inside or out. The whole inside needed to be rebuilt. It took us two years and a lot of work. We knocked down walls, added skylights. We spent weeks just picking the right handles for the kitchen cabinets. Barbara used to say it drove her crazy, how I would go on and on about something like the perfect handles or sink fixtures. But I knew how important it was to do everything right and when we were finished the house was just what we wanted.

We planted hundreds of bulbs, tulips, daffodils and a couple of trees. Barbara used to complain that she was getting washer-woman's knees from kneeling in the dirt all the time. But she loved it. I know that. We painted the house grey-blue and used to laugh at people's reactions when we told them we lived in the blue house on the corner. We went around on that one for months. At first Barbara thought it was too blue but I was trying to get a kind of sky effect and it worked.

We had the most incredible roses. We put a split rail fence along one side of the front yard. Barbara went out and bought rose bushes and put them in while I was at work. She didn't know anything about roses. She didn't know what type to buy for a fence or how to protect them from shock when you plant them. She just dug some holes and put them in. I didn't think they would live. We had a couple of neighbors who said they would never grow on that side of the house because there wasn't enough sun.

The next year those roses came in like a carpet. They never stopped growing. People would stop their cars and come up and ask us what kind of roses they were and what we were using for fertilizer. We used to laugh about that. Barbara didn't even water them as a rule.

When she got pregnant we agreed she would stay home with the baby even if it meant a little belt-tightening. That's what she said she wanted, and I did too. Then, when Ashley is less than a year old, Barbara says she wants to go back to school for her MBA. I said fine, if that's what she wanted. Then she and Dan Green get involved, and in my house. That's what really gets to me. They did it in my house with my child in the house. I don't care what she says.

Gloria met Barbara a few times. One time Barbara fixed her up with a date, someone she knew at the store. He was an accountant and I could see right away he wasn't Gloria's type. He must have been in his thirties, balding. Barbara seemed to think he was good-looking but I didn't see it. Gloria told me later that she thought the reason Barbara picked him was that she liked him herself. She said that's what married women do. They fix up their friends with men they want themselves and then spend the whole night in the kitchen talking to them.

Maybe that's happened to her but I don't think that was the case with Barbara. I don't think she was interested in anyone else at that point. We were still working on the house, she had her job. Things were going well for us. I think she really did pick him for Gloria. She just didn't know Gloria the way I did.

She may have been a little jealous of Gloria. That's what Maureen says, that some women are jealous of their husband's old friends. They want to have a new life together, nothing from the husband's past.

Barbara would say, "How's your cowgirl? Heard from your cowgirl?" She still says it. And when she cut her hair off she said she did it because she didn't want to look like Gloria. That was another thing. I loved her hair long but she kept cutting it and cutting it until it was short as a boy's. Now she says she is growing it again. Women are funny, aren't they?

Maureen is different. We really get along. I can talk to her about anything and nothing bothers her. There is nothing jealous about her. I've told her about all the women I've known and the things we used to do in Mexico. I even told her about the whorehouse and the girl down there. All she did was laugh. She said she was glad I got that kind of thing out of my system. She says she really wants to meet Gloria, that I should ask her out for a visit the next time we talk. Maureen is special that way.

18

L.A. is a good town. People can say whatever they want about LA but it has been good to me. I came here after Barbara and I divorced and I'm glad I made the move. I like the people, the weather. Even with all the problems, the city works. This is where I started dating again.

Linda Thomas was the first real relationship I had after the divorce. We had a great deal in common, both of us lawyers, both in investment law. We dated for almost two years. She was a beautiful woman, long blond hair, beautiful eyes. What happened had nothing to do with her. She was a great gal but I wasn't ready for any type of commitment. I was still very much emotionally involved with Barbara who had already started talking about selling the house. And there was Ashley and trying to figure out how to stay involved in her life. Linda was ready for a long-term commitment. The timing was off. That's all.

In a way I'm sorry we weren't able to go a little further with our relationship. I wanted to keep seeing her but she said it would be too difficult for her. I know she was hurt, but I never led her on. She knew what the situation was when we started dating. It was too soon for me to get involved. I do think about her sometimes and I've thought about calling her to see how she's doing but I don't think that would be fair. I would have liked us to stay friends but men and women don't seem to be able to do that, do they?

Karen was the tough one for me. We actually met through a computer dating service. I never thought I'd do something like that but I was busy with the job and I didn't have time to get out and meet people. This service was for high level professionals. You filled out an extensive questionnaire and then you did a video interview. Karen and I turned out to be a perfect match. We liked the same food, movies, television shows. It was wild.

I was in love with Karen and I was ready to make a commitment to our relationship. My parents liked her. My father called her ballsy, a great compliment coming from him. She had her opinions but she knew how to defer to him, something Barbara never learned.

They met her out here in L.A. and Karen and I went over to the show in Santa Fe to see them. We had a great time. Then I took her to Sedona for a weekend. Everything was fine as far as I could see but she called it off right after that. Something could have happened that weekend but I can't figure out what. Being with someone else's parents can be tough, but Mother is always nice and my father was on relatively good behavior. We had a couple of nice meals. We took walks together. Gloria came up one night. A typical Sedona weekend, quiet.

Then, on the flight back to L.A. Karen said she thought it would be better if we cooled it for a while. She said she needed some space. I must have asked her a hundred times if it was something I had done, if I had done or said something wrong. She said no, she just wanted a break. When I asked her for how long she wouldn't give me a straight answer.

I called her every day. I went over to the apartment. I tried to make her talk about what was wrong. All she would say was that it wasn't working for her, that it wasn't fun. That was it; it wasn't fun. She wanted to end the relationship and there was nothing I could say. Here we are in love one day in Sedona, Arizona and the next day she can't even talk to me. It was almost like Barbara all over again except Karen and I were just starting and I did want to know what she needed, what she wanted. I cared. I was asking the questions.

That's the one positive thing about divorce. You can learn from a divorce, take a look at the mistakes you might have made. I didn't want to make mistakes with Karen. I kept thinking I must be missing something about what was going on, missing something about her.

I talked to my friends. I talked to Gloria. I thought maybe she had noticed something that weekend. With my father, you never know. But Gloria didn't see anything. She said maybe it was because she was there, that we had been talking too much about old times. I don't buy that. Karen knew Gloria was coming and she was only there for one night. How difficult could that have been? No, it wasn't Gloria or my father or anything that happened in Sedona. I think she was planning to break it off before we got there.

Gloria once told me that when a woman decides its over, for whatever reason, that's it. She doesn't come back no matter what you do because she's already been thinking about leaving for a long time. For her, it's finished. Maybe that's true but good did come out of the breakup. If Karen hadn't called it quits, I never would have met Maureen. And, that's important.

I always tell Maureen I picked her out right away. She says no, she did the picking and had been up in the office a few times before I noticed her. She was a friend of the wife of one of my partners. I saw her at the office and asked him about her. He and his wife had me over to dinner to meet her. We've been dating every since and it is working out well for both of us. She's younger but it doesn't make any difference. Even my father is impressed by her and the way she thinks. He said she's a very level-headed young woman. She is also a Ronald Reagan-George Bush Republican so there are no shouting matches over dinner. Thank God.

We agree right down the line on politics. I am a conservative like my father although I am not as vocal or dogmatic as he is. I never went through any period of youthful rebellion where sons are supposed to break away from their parents by becoming the opposite of their fathers. No, the closest thing I had to a rebellion was that year I went to Mexico, and then living with Marjorie for three years. I was never part of any counterculture. I didn't march in the '70s. I didn't do drugs. I drank, yes, and still do. But I have never equated a few beers on a Sunday afternoon or a glass of wine at dinner to a heroin addiction. That's the way the liberals do it, blurring the lines so eventually we're supposed to say all drugs should be legalized. Ridiculous.

The only experience I had with any kind of drugs was the time I went down to Tennessee to see Paul Monroe. That was one crazy weekend. Marjorie had left for New York and I needed to get away from Chicago for a few days so I drove down there to see Paul. I hadn't seen him since Mexico. He lived in this small town in the middle of a farming area, the kind of place where people would sit on their front porches at night. Very American.

Paul was working in the family insurance business with his mother. The father had either died or left them years before. Paul never talked about him. Paul was also growing marijuana in the hills outside of town. That surprised me. We never got into grass in Mexico. A lot of people did but not in our group. We were the drinkers.

Some of those plants must have been seven feet tall. He was using cow manure from the local dairy as fertilizer. He went out every day to take care of them. We went up there and shook each of the plants so the females and the males would exchange pollen. Paul knew everything about growing marijuana. He wasn't selling it. He was using it.

Now you have to remember, this is the South in the '70s. Down there you could end up in jail for doing anything, and certainly for growing marijuana. There were people in Texas, probably still are, who were thrown into jail for having a mari-

juana seed in their car. , I was sure some sheriff
named Bubba was going to jump out of the bushes
and grab us both. That would be the end of any law
career I had planned. I kept thinking about that
movie with Paul Newman where he ends up on the
chain gang for robbing a parking meter. But Monroe said we didn't have to worry, the sheriff was a
friend of the family and would probably warn him
if anyone decided to do something about the pot
plants. That didn't help much. I was still scared
most of the time.

Boy, did we get ripped that weekend. His pot
was incredible. He said it was the cow shit. It was
something. We did everything you hear about, the
eating jags, the bags of candy. We tried to cook
something but lost interest halfway through. We
almost killed each other when Paul decided we had
to go squirrel hunting. The squirrels were safe that
weekend. We only had one rifle between us, which
probably saved our lives. Every time one of us shot
it we both fell down on the ground laughing. I had
a bruise on my shoulder for a year from the kick of
that gun.

We walked through the town stoned out of
our minds. We said hello to everybody sitting on
their porches. I was sure they knew we were stoned
but Paul said they didn't know what marijuana
was. He said they were Baptists and didn't know
what liquor was.

Something else surprised me that weekend:
Paul's financial situation. I assumed he came from
money. In Mexico we all lived well. Nobody worried about money, as far I knew. Paul's mother had

a nice little house and the business. Paul lived over the office. He had a good set-up but I could see there wasn't much money around. Not that it mattered, but I was a little surprised.

I did ask him what had happened between Gloria and him but all he would say was that she was a bitch and had screwed him over. I let it drop. They should never have been together in the first place, that's what I always thought.

I always worried about her. I know it sounds chauvinistic but I always thought what Gloria needed was a good man. I wanted to see her happy. There have been times when I wanted to make life easier for her. I've thought about offering her money, saying, "Here's five hundred, a thousand, take a vacation, come out to visit." But I know she wouldn't take it. Besides, if Gloria needs anything she has her family. I am sure her father helps her out. There may even be a trust fund from her mother's estate. There is money there. Besides, Gloria likes being a survivor.

There has always been a kind of hardness about her. I don't think she lets herself care about things, about people, the way other people do. Look at the relationship with Paul. They were together, what, two years, three years? And when it's over she doesn't say a word. I didn't find out for at least a year. She acted like it was no big deal. Maybe it wasn't to her. She's that way about a lot of things. She doesn't care about much or she pretends she doesn't. She's very good if she is pretending.

Look at that day in Mexico. I don't think she

was the least bit afraid, not the way I was. I was scared shitless and I don't care who knows it. I thought somebody was going to pull a knife on us and there was a damn good chance of that happening, I can tell you that. I think we both tend to gloss over the fact that we could have been badly hurt that day, especially Paul and I. It may sound like an exaggeration but I think we could have been killed. Things like that happen all the time down there. People get trampled to death at soccer matches, tourists disappear and usually the cops are involved in some way. It wasn't safe down there. Mexico was never safe.

We heard all the stories. There were a couple of American students they arrested for robbing a gas station. It was ridiculous. They didn't rob any gas station. They were in jail for weeks and we heard they were tortured. There was a picture of them on the front page of one of the papers when they got out and they did look messed up. They looked terrible. We heard it cost their parents twenty or thirty thousand to get them out.

I knew a guy who was picked up by the Mexican police near the border in Nuevo Laredo. Supposedly, he bought marijuana to take back to the States. But I knew the guy. He didn't smoke pot. He was a drinker. His family paid ten thousand to get him out of jail. We knew the cops had planted the stuff. That's what they did. They would plant it in the car. Then they'd pick you up, put you in jail until you paid them off. The word down there was to go through your car with a fine-tooth comb before you got near the border and then not stop again until you were across.

Some of the guys used to say Mexico would be a great place if it weren't for the Mexicans. I didn't like that. Bad things did happen down there, but most of the time the Mexicans were great. That one day, what happened that day, was an aberration.

It was a like a fair at first, people selling food, laughing, yelling at each other. It was always that way down there, people having a good time. There wasn't any hatred toward us. Gloria is wrong about that. They didn't dislike us that day or any other day. Mexicans are very friendly people. That day was totally out of the ordinary for them and us.

Gloria always says we were being blamed for something, that the people felt cheated because the man had died so they took it out on us. I don't agree at all. I don't think anyone can explain what happened that day. It was the first and only time I felt any anger from the Mexicans and it wasn't from everybody. Only a few men on the road bothered us. Of course, that was bad enough.

I don't think Gloria realizes that those men weren't only following us. They were actually bumping up against me, pushing me. One of them was yelling in my ear but I didn't understand what he was saying. All they wanted me or Paul to do was to make one mistake, one false move, then they would have gone for us. Joe Pajorski was right about that. If he had made one move to protect Becks, it would have been very bad. The same for us. If I had tripped over a rock or fallen down or if I had made any kind of motion for them to move back, they might have gone for us. Yes, I was scared. You bet I was scared.

I remember how hot it was that day. The sweat was rolling down my face. I remember that. They were all looking at me, close to me, with those big smiles of theirs, just waiting. I was trying to look like nothing was bothering me. You couldn't show fear. You had to hold yourself in. That was even more frightening. You had to look like everything was fine. Smile, even.

I wasn't worried about Gloria, not much. I knew if anybody was going to be hurt it would be Paul or me or both of us. I used to have this mental picture of how she would react if we had been hurt. I can see her kneeling in the road the way that girl did at Kent State, her arms raised, crying out. I know that really isn't the way she would have acted. Not Gloria. She would have turned around to the crowd and told them to get away from us. Nothing would have scared her. In my fantasy though, I see her kneeling and holding my head and telling me everything is going to be okay.

Of course, luckily, nothing like that happened. We ended up in the church. I remember that perfectly. The church was very dark inside and cool and quiet. There were some stained-glass windows but most of the light was coming from all of these candles that were burning, hundreds of candles. The light inside that church was almost golden with those candles, a golden light. That was a beautiful church.

I don't know how we found it. It almost seems as though we fell into it, that we were standing against this wall and then we suddenly fell through the doors into the church. We stayed there about thirty minutes and then went back to the city.

There is a lot about that day I don't remember and I don't see why I should try to. I don't like to talk about that day. It's the kind of story that can upset people. I remember how upset Linda was after hearing Gloria and me talk about it in Sedona. She told me later she couldn't believe I had seen something like that and wasn't changed somehow. She said it would have changed her life and seemed to be upset when I told her I didn't think it had changed mine.

She said, or maybe it was Karen who said there was something wrong with me because I didn't care about that man dying. That's crazy. What was I supposed to do, stop it? How? We couldn't do that. All we could do was get away. People who've never lived in a place like Mexico don't understand how it is. It's their country. You don't get involved. If you do, you get hurt.

I think it was Karen who said things like that had never happened to her and she didn't like knowing about them. She wasn't feeling well that weekend at my parents and I don't suppose having to listen to my father and Gloria fight helped. I had forgotten about that. They had a good one that night.

My father was on one of his favorite topics, talking about how the Indians treated their captives, how captives prayed the men would get to them before the women because the women were so much crueler. I always find it interesting that a man who has spent his life painting pictures sympathetic to the American Indian can get so much pleasure talking about the horrible things they did.

Gloria, always the liberal, wasn't about to let it pass. She said the whites in this country had their own history of inflicting pain. Her theory was that we didn't do as much of it as the Indians because we got bored easily and wanted to move on to something else. My father said that while we might have a lynch mob every so often, we still didn't take the same kind of pleasure the Indians got out of barbecuing a prisoner alive. Gloria told him he needed to check that out with some of the blacks in this country. Gloria can be good. She might have been a good lawyer.

This was the night he called her a bitch. Mother and I were in the kitchen laughing. We were used to their fights but it couldn't have been easy for Karen. Still, that isn't what set her off. She already knew what she was going to do. I see that now. Nothing I could have said or done that weekend would have made any difference at all. Karen had her own agenda.

I haven't seen Gloria in quite a while. We've talked a few times but that's all. My life has been too busy. Even when I've been in Sedona, there hasn't been the opportunity to connect with her. She lives in Dallas now, and with her father in San Diego she doesn't get over to Arizona. Besides, she can really be too much sometimes.

I haven't seen Paul since that trip to Tennessee. I haven't tried to call to find out if he's still there. I probably should. He was a good guy. I'd like to know what he's been up to. But men lose touch with old friends. We move on. It's the women who keep in touch. They hold it together, don't they, friendships, families. Men have to keep moving ahead. Which is sad in a way. But things change and, like Maureen says, you can't hold on to the past.

19

I think my relationship with Maureen could be a very serious one. That she is younger doesn't matter at all. She is smart and talented. She works for one of the best decorators in the Valley. She has the career if she wants it but she also has strong feelings about family and how children should be raised. She believes a woman should stay at home with the children until they are old enough for school and then she thinks the mother should be in the house when the child gets home in the afternoon. I feel the same way. A mother should be able to stay home if there is enough money. If there isn't, perhaps they shouldn't have children.

I've never been against women having a career but I think a child needs his mother and more women are going back to the home to take care of their children. You can't blame them. It's not easy out there, not for men or women.

That Maureen and I share the same values and beliefs is very important to me. Anyone who has been married will tell you that the passion, the sex, the excitement dies down after the first few years. You have to be with someone who is like you. You need that similarity of backgrounds and values. Barbara and I had mutual interests, especially with the house and Ashley, but we didn't really agree on many things. I see that now. That had a lot to do with what happened to us. The sexual excitement calmed down, then the baby came and then she decides she wants out. It is not that unusual.

Barbara was looking for that excitement with Dan Green. She never understood that marriages aren't supposed to be exciting. Marriage isn't about high-charged sex and constant excitement. Being married is not supposed to be an adventure a minute. You calm down, do what has to be done, make a life together. If Barbara had understood that I think we could have worked things out. I was willing. She was the one who wasn't committed to making the marriage work. Maybe my father is right. Maybe what she wanted was a way out of Chicago. But as to any commitment to me or our marriage, I don't see it.

I think that's one of the reasons Gloria has never been married or in any kind of long-term relationship. I don't think she knows how to commit either. I can't think of anything she's ever been committed to, or anyone. Not really. She seems to pick men totally on the basis of passion. That one guy I met in Dallas didn't have anything in common with her. That's why her relationships never last, no similarity, no commitment.

Of course, Gloria would probably find all of that very boring. She would think a healthy relationship, like the one I have with Maureen, would have to be dull. She wants the excitement too, all the problems and the chaos. You can't even have a simple conversation with Gloria without it turning into a battle of some kind and one she has to win. We disagree on almost everything. Politically, she is one of those liberals who believes everybody should be allowed to do their own thing and everybody else should be forced to pay for them doing it.

She was against Viet Nam, of course. She says it was stupid, a blood bath. She sent me a postcard saying how nice it was that we can now sell Coca-Cola in Hanoi. All right, it was handled badly but our commitment wasn't wrong. We were doing the right thing for the right reasons. What we lacked was the support of the people like Gloria who didn't understand what we were trying to do. We were trying to protect a people and prevent the growth of Communism in Southeast Asia. We should have fought to win. That was our mistake in Viet Nam. But we learned from it. Look at Panama, Granada, Desert Storm.

I don't think Gloria or any liberal is willing to see the complications of the world we live in today. Yes, we have supported some terrible people but we do it because the alternative is worse. Gloria wants a world where everything is black and white. It doesn't work that way. There are too many gray areas in life.

I think one of the major differences between Republican and Democratic administrations in the past thirty years is that Republicans understand that, especially in foreign policy. They deal with the gray areas. The government of Kuwait might not have been the most democratic or admirable in its treatment of foreign nationals or women but we had to support them over Hussein. He was worse. Sound foreign policy has to be based on the ability to deal with the gray areas, to make the compromises necessary for the overall good.

This is something we have had to deal with constantly in Latin America, supporting right-wing governments with terrible track records on human rights. But the alternative is worse, left-wing terrorists. You can't always find the saint in politics. You have to go with what is best for your country and your country's interests. I want a president and a Congress who think like that. We've had a few and they've been Republican. I also want a president and a Congress willing to stand firm once they've chosen their position. Reagan did that and so did George Bush.

Could Bill Clinton or Jimmy Carter have pulled off Desert Storm? No. In Carter's case, he was always too concerned with doing the right thing for all involved. You can't operate that way in today's world. As for Clinton, name me one strong stand he ever took about anything. The question has to be, in time of war or national emergency, what kind of man do you want leading this country, a Ronald Reagan or a Bill Clinton?

Gloria is one of those people who are always talking about how dumb Reagan was, how he slept his way through the presidency. I think history is going to prove Ronald Reagan was one of the greatest presidents this country ever had. Communism fell under Reagan, the Wall came down. The Reagan-Bush years were great for this country. We are still enjoying the benefits and we are still fighting to keep them.

Our economic growth was incredible in the Reagan-Bush years. Those years were great for many people, myself included. A lot of people began their financial growth because of those Republican policies. Under Ronald Reagan, we were finally back to operating on the philosophy this country was built on, that government is not supposed to be in the business of running our business or our lives. People should be responsible for their own successes or failures.

We are still fighting that battle. It comes up in every argument over health care and social security and welfare and Medicare. When was it decided that we were supposed to support people from birth to death in this country? Whatever happened to personal responsibility?

I am tired of paying for a system that supports teenage girls having three and four children with no fathers. I am tired of the drug addicts and the drunks and the bums with their hands out all the time. I am tired of being told that I am supposed to pay and pay and pay for people who won't take care of themselves.

Of course there are problems in this country. It isn't always easy to get a job, especially without the education. But I pay for the education. How am I at fault if someone doesn't want one. The system works for those who are willing to work.

A lot of people in this country still haven't woken up to the fact that our economic base has shifted. There are no more cradle-to-coffin jobs. We have to compete on a global level now. We have a massive economic block developing throughout Asia and another one with the economic unification of Europe. They don't only offer new market potential for American goods; they are our competition. In many cases, they can produce goods faster, cheaper and better than we can.

There is no more room in this country for unions that want secure jobs with more money and less work. There is a limit to how much businesses can pay out and still survive. Of course we are moving operations out of the country. Of course we're taking advantage of cheap labor. We have to. Our workers have priced themselves out of their jobs. In business, it is the bottom line that counts. No profit, no business. People can yell all they want about companies moving south or using cheap labor in Asia but that doesn't change the reality that the business of business is making money.

Many of us prepared for this kind of future. My own firm is an example of what a lot of good business minds did right in the '80s. We saw how the economics of the world was changing and we did something about it. We started building a client base interested in development and investment outside of the United States. We also started working with some Japanese companies making moves into California and the Pacific Northwest. I really enjoy the Japanese clients. I've learned a great deal about business from them. They are shrewd. They don't plan in five-year increments. They plan fifty years in advance. That is what we should be doing in this country.

Many of our American clients have investments in Europe and Asia. We are not so hot about Latin America, regardless of any tax benefits. Without stable government and a strong middle class, there is too much potential for problems. I've had people ask me about investing in Mexico, in the maquiladoras along the border or prime development property along the coast, even about building vacation homes with part-time rental potential. I'll give them the benefits but I will also give them some personal advice. And that is to be very, very careful.

You simply don't know what is going to happen down there, what that government will do. They could easily turn around and say everything you've built here, all your investments, all your holdings, your money in the bank, it all belongs to us now. Think it couldn't happen? Ask the British about the railroads they built. Talk to Americans and Mexicans about Mexican banks. Their own people have lost millions, billions.

The problems down there are terrible. The oil industry, which could have provided a sound economic base for their entire economy, is a disaster. The unemployment is unbelievable and corruption is everywhere and at every level. It was bad enough twenty years ago. Everyone had to be paid off. If you parked your car on the street you had to pay some kid to watch it. It you didn't, he would steal the hubcaps or the radio. I can't imagine what it's like now.

Of course, the real problem is population growth. Mexico has one of the highest in the world. The people have no money and no jobs but they continue to have five and six children. This country has been Mexico's safety valve for overpopulation for decades but it can't go on much longer. I am certainly not the only one saying that. Talk to anyone living here in southern California or in any of the border states. Illegal immigration is out of control out here. It is affecting every aspect of our lives.

They are crossing the border by the thousands. You see videos of them walking across in broad daylight. There have been news reports of groups of them rushing the border guards, just running across. The women are coming here to have their babies. We are paying for that. You can hardly blame them, wanting the best health care for their children, but that isn't the only reason. Those babies become immediate citizens of this country and eligible for all the benefits.

In a lot of ways, illegal immigrants are getting more help then our own citizens get. It doesn't make any sense. I hate to say this but there is going to be a backlash. People aren't going to put up with this much longer. Of course, any politician who says anything about the need to control immigration is accused of being a racist. The age of political correctness.

People in this country are going to have to face up to the fact that this is a tough world. We can't let in everyone who is unhappy or poor. That kind of immigration only worked when the land was still wide open, when we needed people to settle and farm and to build the railroads and work in the factories. That isn't the case anymore. We have our own problems to deal with now. We can't afford millions of immigrants coming in every year untrained, no education. What are they supposed to do? Most of my friends agree with me on this one. They believe, as I do, that we need to get some common sense back into our government. You can't do for everybody, not anymore.

Maureen and I have been making some new friends at the church we've been going to, people who share a lot of our beliefs. There it is again, that similarity of values and beliefs. They are professional people, like us. Some of the wives have put their careers on hold to stay home with their children. I enjoy these people and I like the church.

I hadn't been in church for years. We were raised Lutheran and my father used to take us to church every Sunday. He made it the usual ordeal. He would be yelling at all of us to get ready and get in the car. He couldn't stand being late. I never saw that he got any great pleasure out of going to church. He did seem to enjoy making us go, Christina and me. I think he was easier on Billy once Christina and I were out of the house.

I started going again this year, not to a Lutheran church but a non-denominational Christian church. Our faith is based on the teachings of Christ. We don't believe in a literal translation of the Bible. We're not fundamentalists. Nothing like that. But we do accept the Bible as our guide and Jesus Christ as the son of God. In our church, we try to live, in our hearts, the life Jesus preached.

Maureen introduced me to the church. She was raised Episcopalian but she's not comfortable with the recent changes, their relaxed attitude on homosexuality in particular. She didn't believe the church was representing her own values anymore.

We both like the pastor, John Brickston. He's a nice guy, young, bright and quite a salesman. It didn't take him any time at all to get me on two church committees, building and finance, and all the guys seem happy they have a lawyer working with them. I am also taking Bible classes one night a week.

I am comfortable with my faith. I don't use that line about having a personal relationship with Jesus Christ but I do believe in his teachings and the impact they have had on my own life in recent months. I don't share these feelings with everyone, not my business associates or my parents. I am not the type to be talking about my religion to people who don't believe as I do. But my faith is important to me and maybe I should share it at some point.

Of course, I can imagine what someone like Gloria would say. I get defensive even thinking about her reaction. I can see her rolling her eyes and telling me how ridiculous it all is. She'd go on and on about all the terrible things religion has done, all the wars and the way women have been treated, and the poor.

I know the arguments. I've used them myself. But there is a new type of Christianity in the world today, one that does live the word of Christ. Besides, good things have been done because of Christianity. The teachings of Christ have given us a pattern for life, a plan. We can choose to do what we wish with our lives, but there is a path there for us to follow.

That makes me angry, the thought I would have to defend myself to Gloria. Why should I? If my Christian beliefs are important to me and make me a better person, that should be enough for anybody. But not for Gloria. She'd have to say something.

I know she'd bring up that day in Mexico. She always does. She'd say everything that happened that day was because of religion. In a way, she is right but that wasn't true Christianity. That was Mexican Catholicism and that is entirely different. That religion is based on paganism, the old Aztec religion. The Spanish knew the easy way to convert people. They substituted one religion for another. They built their churches on top of the old Aztec pyramids. Spanish Catholicism had the same blood-letting rituals of the Aztecs. How far was the drinking of Christ's blood and the eating of the body of Christ from the Aztec sacrifices? The Aztec priests used to eat human hearts. We've talked about this in Bible class, how Christianity was diluted in the past, how it absorbed other religious practices for expediency's sake.

No, what we saw in Mexico wasn't a religious event. It was what I said before, a fair, a festival. Besides, I don't think about that day. The subject only comes up when Gloria is around. The only reason my parents know anything about it is because Gloria talked about it one night in Sedona.

I still have feelings for Gloria but they aren't as strong as they used to be. There were times in Sedona when I would lay in bed and wait for her, thinking that maybe she would come in to talk to me. I used to think about sneaking in to her room to see her. I never did. I think one of the main reasons I still feel attracted to her is because the whole thing between us was never resolved. If I had gotten her into bed that night in Mexico, I think our relationship would be different right now, if it existed at all. I probably wouldn't still have fantasies about her.

We were close to it that night, whether she wants to admit it or not. I had her blouse undone, her bra unhooked. I had my hands on her breasts and up her skirt. She was responding. There's no doubt about that. I wanted to keep going but she stopped me. She was worried about Paul. She wouldn't even let me drive her home. She took the champagne and got a cab.

She says she doesn't remember anything about that night. I don't believe her. She must remember something but she says she was drunk and only remembers going to the party upstairs.

I still worry about her sometimes, knowing how she lives and how she never thinks about what could happen to her. That train idea of hers is a perfect example. She got it into her head that she wanted to go to Mexico on the train by herself. I blew up at her. It was so typical of how she thinks. Somebody could have grabbed her at some small station and that would have been the end of her. It's bad enough nobody knows where she is when she's in this country. Going to Mexico on a train alone would be crazy. I wouldn't go back there at all, by train or plane.

It's not because I didn't like it down there. I did like Mexico. Every day was an adventure. Mexico was a beautiful country, so full of life. I know part of that was because it was so foreign to all of us. But it also has to do with the people. They could be happy under the worst conditions. There was poverty, sure, but the people always seemed to have something to sell, some kind of business going on. They were hard-working people and very proud. They had this sense of beauty. Even the poorest house on the road to Acapulco would have pots of flowers around it.

I was taking pictures back then. Some days I was shooting three or four rolls of film. I was taking pictures of everything, children, buildings, animals. There was this one shot I took on the way to Acapulco. We stopped so someone could pee and I got out to take some pictures of this hut near the road. There was a dog standing outside and then this little boy appeared in the doorway. He was wearing a tee-shirt and nothing else. It was the way the light hit him, the darkness behind him and then the frame of the doorway. Right then he smiled at me and the dog looked at him. A great shot.

I don't take pictures like that anymore. The camera I have now does everything by itself. I don't know where the old camera is. I think I left it in Evergreen with a box of pictures and other things from Mexico when Marjorie and I stopped there on our way to Chicago. I don't know where that box is now but I suppose Mother has it put away somewhere. She saves everything. I wouldn't mind taking a look at those pictures again to see if I was any good. I actually thought about being a photographer for a living, staying down there and shooting pictures for U.S. magazines. Just a dream.

I did try to go back once a few years ago, but

only as far as the border. Karen and I went down to Tijuana so she could do some shopping. We parked the car on the Mexican side and got out. Then I got this strange feeling. I felt danger. I felt like something bad was going to happen if we didn't get out of there right that minute. It may have been all the noise and the people on the streets and the car horns. The merchants were yelling and pulling at people. There was that thick smell that Mexico always had, the diesel fuel and cooking fires, food. All of a sudden I felt overwhelmed and I did have this sense of danger. Nothing like that ever happened to me before or since, like a premonition.

I said to Karen, "Get back in the car. We have to go. We don't want to stay." It must have been the way I said it or the way I looked but she didn't say a word. She got back into the car and we left. We were back across the border in about ten minutes. I felt fine the minute we crossed over. No matter what you say about this country, all the problems we have here, I feel safe here. I always have.

20

Of course, I haven't forgotten that day in Mexico. There are parts of that day I will never forget, like the man who was carrying the stretcher. I still remember his face. That's how much I was affected by what happened. There were four of them carrying that stretcher and I'll never forget the man in front who passed next to me.

I remember all of their eyes. They had those flat brown eyes, the kind you can't see into. They were wearing army uniforms, green combat clothes with those high-laced black boots you see when soldiers march in parades.

This one man though, I saw him clearly because he came so close to me. He was heavy, built big but not fat, although there may have been some belly there. He had that thick black Mexican hair and some of it was hanging down over his forehead. It was falling into his eyes. He was running hard. They were all running hard up that hill. I don't remember there being much of an expression on his face. He just looked intent. But when he came back down I could see how worried he looked. I could see that.

I would say he was in his mid-thirties. He probably had a big family, four or five kids and a heavy wife who laughed a lot and who wore her hair in braids. I bet his children loved him. He was probably a man who went to church, Catholic like most Mexicans. That's how I see him. Maybe he didn't go every Sunday but when he did, he prayed on his knees. And now, here he is, carrying a man on a stretcher who was supposed to be Christ. He would have seen him on the cross when it was back on the ground. He had to have.

He had a nice enough face, round, dark skin, like a million other Mexican faces. But I don't care. If I had any artistic ability at all, I could draw that face right now. That's how well I remember it. I could work with a police artist and come up with a perfect sketch of that man's face. Not only that. I know that even now, more than twenty years later, if I saw that man again and if he was worried about something, I would recognize him. Yes, I would. Partly it was the eyes when he came back down. They were frightened. You could see fear in his eyes.

When they came back down the hill they were running but they weren't going as fast as they had on the way up because now they had the man on the stretcher and they were on an incline so they had to hold themselves back. They were stumbling, sliding on the loose rocks. But what did it matter then, to run like that? I wonder about that even now. If the man was dead, why did they have to run down the hill?

Maybe they wanted the people to think he was still alive, that he was being rushed to some hospital. But his face was covered so he must have been dead. I thought he was dead. So did everyone else.

That man with the stretcher was so close I could look right into his face. I would have been able to see if he was sweating but he wasn't. He was grim. That's the only word I can think of, grim. The stretcher must have been heavy. That would account for part of the way he looked but there was more. He looked so worried, not frightened, I don't mean that. I mean worried, worried.

I've never talked about that man but that doesn't mean I didn't care. That I remember his face so clearly all these years shows how much I cared. He was so human. That was the thing. He looked the way any of us would if we were in his position. I would have looked exactly like that. He also looked like he knew something more than we did about what was going on. The only thing I can think of is that the man was still alive. He could have been. But I still don't know why that would be important if everyone already thought he was dead.

The priest said it over the loudspeaker, that he was dead. I couldn't understand him but Gloria said he was talking about how the man was only a symbol and they shouldn't be upset over what had happened. How could he have said something like that? Of course they were going to be upset.

I don't remember certain parts of the day. I don't remember the rock-throwing on the mountain or the part about the little boy getting hurt. I remember the part in the field so well because that's where I started to get nervous. I could see there were too many people. It was like a scene out of Gandhi, thousands of people waiting to hear him speak. I wish I had a camera but Gloria was right when she told us not to bring them. I can't imagine what would have happened to us if we had started taking pictures.

I don't remember seeing the Romans or the cross moving the way Gloria says she does but I didn't have to. I knew what was going to happen. I had already looked behind me while Gloria and Paul were watching the road. I was so shocked by what I saw I couldn't tell them. I saw the two men hanging on their crosses, the thieves. I couldn't believe it. There they were, strapped up on their crosses with ropes. They weren't nailed. They had ropes around their arms and chests tying them to the crosses. I think they may have had a little seat under their butts so they weren't hanging there without any support. I am almost sure they did.

One of them moved his head from side to side like he wanted to get loose and the other one was talking to someone standing below the cross who I couldn't see. Then someone passed him up a water or wine pouch on the end of a pole. The man on the cross shook his head like he didn't want it.

They were little men, tiny little men, mixed Indian and Spanish blood probably, skinny arms and legs. I don't know how many other people were up on the hill but you got the feeling that there was a lot of commotion going on up there, people moving around, talking. That's why I must have missed the Romans and the cross. I was watching the hill.

Gloria and I have never talked about the thieves or about the hammering. That's what happened next. At first, I didn't know what it was. The sound didn't register. Remember, I hadn't seen the cross on the road so I didn't put it all together right away. I heard something that sounded as though someone was up there hammering a tent peg into the ground. They were hammering and hammering and other people seemed to be talking, like they were giving them instructions. I couldn't see this but I have this vision of men squatting down and giving the people with the hammers instructions.

God, I break into a sweat just thinking about that hammering sound. The whole thing took so damn long, that's the thing. It took so long. I'm thinking, get it over with, you bastards, get it over with. And even then I wasn't admitting to myself what it was they were doing. Part of me knew but the other part only wanted them to get it over with.

It was like dry thumps but you could hear that metal-on-metal pinging and then it was muffled as though the nail was going into something soft. God, what a fucking nightmare. I think that's when I grabbed Gloria and said, "We've got to get out of here," but nobody moved.

You know, I am not sure I actually saw the man on the cross. I can sort of see it, the cross, when Gloria describes how it came into view above us but the man has never been clear in my mind. It was as though there was this black form on the cross. It was as though the sun blinded me right as the cross came up. It all happened so fast. The next thing we knew the men with the stretcher were running past us.

I do remember what Paul said when we were

all looking up at the cross or where the cross had been. I can smile now when I think about it because he said, clear as a bell, "Jesus Christ." Yes.

I started to tell John Brickston about that day. We were working outside the church on the sprinkler system and I started to tell him how I had seen some strange things in Mexico with their religion. I was saying how so much of their Catholicism seemed to involve pain and suffering but John misunderstood. He thought I meant New Mexico and he started talking about the penitentes, the men who do the self-flagellation, the whippings, the thorns through their flesh. I didn't correct him. I let it drop. I wouldn't know how to tell him about what we saw. Why would I tell him?

There were years when I never thought about that day, not once. For a while I thought it was some kind of dream, that it hadn't really happened as I remembered it. We didn't even talk much about it when we got back to the city. There was already a party going on by the time we got back to Paul's, one of our usual drunks. All of the people who had been with us had a few war stories to tell but mostly we laughed because it all seemed so strange. Gloria told everyone how we ran into the church with her yelling "Sanctuary, sanctuary." Joe told us how they went after Becks on the road down the hill. But poor O'Brien got the worst of it. He always did.

He was one of those big Irish guys you always like. He was from some farm town in Nebraska or North or South Dakota. He was always drinking too much and getting into trouble. He sure had a hell of a time of it that day. When we went up the road he stayed in some cantina drinking beer and waiting for us to come back.

Somehow he missed us or he thought he had so he went to get his car to go home. When he got to his car, all four tires were flat. He couldn't speak much Spanish, and where was he going to get four tires fixed on a Mexican holiday? We had to laugh. Things like that were always happening to him.

I don't remember Paul and Gloria and me talking about what we had seen. Not then. And I didn't talk about it for a long time afterwards. But that doesn't mean we didn't care. Of course we cared. Nobody is that tough, not even Gloria.

It was a horrible experience and it did make an impression on me. Whoever said it didn't was wrong. I did care about that man, the one who died. We all did. But everything happened so fast. We were in a state of shock and we were worried about our own safety. There was nothing we could have done even if we had wanted to. Of course I cared about what happened to that man. The whole thing was a nightmare, being chased, running. You don't forget something like that.

I can't even watch *Spartacus*. Whenever I see it on television I click past as fast as I can. I am always afraid I am going to see that part at the end, the road with all the men on the crosses still moving. God, that's a horrible death. I don't need to see that again.

21

My father took out life insurance policies on all of us when we were kids. When Billy died he divided the insurance between Christina and me. I didn't like taking the money and I promised myself that I would invest it in some way that would involve Billy's memory. I was going to put the money aside and eventually build it into a fund in his name. I was going to use it to make contributions to charities he would have liked. That was the plan.

In the beginning, that ten thousand was the only money I had to invest so I did keep careful records, but then I started making my own investments and the investments I made with Billy's money were absorbed into my general portfolio. That's the way it stands now and it bothers me sometimes.

Sometimes I feel as though I should have kept the money completely separate, but there were advantages in combining the investments. In the end, the whole account profited, his money and mine. I do make contributions every year in his name. I pick groups that usually involve kids and sports. He would have liked that. I give at least five hundred dollars a year in his name. I've also been thinking about getting my accountant to do a computer chase on the original ten thousand. Maybe he could come up with some kind of estimate of what that initial investment would be worth now and we could somehow cull out a certain amount and really establish a separate fund. I've thought about that and I think it would make me feel better.

It was very bad when he died, very bad. He was on his way back to college from spring break in Mexico. He and his friends had gone down there to do some partying and scuba diving. They got hit by a drunk driver just outside of Phoenix. There were two other kids with him, a girl and the guy who was driving. They both survived but Billy was riding shotgun and took the full impact of the other car. The driver was coming into traffic from the on-ramp and smashed into them. He rolled his car and died a couple of days later. That's as much as the police could say. They called my father and he told Mother and then called Christina and me. I was in Chicago with Marjorie. It was an awful shock.

He was such a nice kid. He was always interested in everything, all kinds of sports, baseball, football. He loved animals. He always had a dog or a cat around him. There was one time when he told Mother he was going to get a monkey. That didn't last. He was good-looking, like my father, tall, lanky. The girls loved him but I believe he liked his sports better. Christina says he was the best of the bunch but we don't talk about him much, not at any length. I think that's natural. Mother may mention him on his birthday. She'll call and say this would have been Billy's such and such birthday. My father doesn't talk about him at all.

Maureen says I shouldn't let this thing with

Billy's money bother me. She says in reality it was always Father's money. He was the beneficiary. She thinks like I do, that Billy would like what I am doing with the contributions. Maureen says I should do whatever I think is fair but she says I have no reason to feel guilty.

That's the way she is, very understanding about what I go through and very thoughtful. She found an old picture of Billy in one of my law school books. I had forgotten all about the picture. He is in his high school football uniform with Christina on one side and me on the other. Maureen is having it professionally reproduced and she bought a silver frame for it. She is going to give it to Mother for Christmas. That will mean a lot to Mother.

She was hit very hard by Billy's death. She spent a lot of time in her room or walking alone and that lasted for quite a while. But, my father didn't change his patterns at all. He went into the studio every day and painted. I know he was painting because at night I would go in and look at what he had done. He was working on his first large canvas, a painting called "Dawn of the Hunt." It wasn't about death or anything sad. That's what you'd think he'd be doing. No, it was a painting of Indians preparing for a buffalo hunt, getting their horses and their weapons ready. At the next show in Santa Fe that painting sold to a museum in Kansas for one hundred thousand dollars. It was the highest price ever paid for Western art from a living artist. The story ran in all the papers including the *New York Times*. This was right at the beginning of the Western art craze that really hit this country in the '80s.

What still amazes me about that painting is the lack of any indication that my father had lost his son at about the same time he was working on it. They used the painting on the poster for the next show and I kept one. I've looked at it often. I can't see any hint of death or rebirth in it. I looked for that when I was sneaking into his studio every night the week after Billy died. If there is a sense of loss in that painting, I can't see it, but the death must have affected my father terribly because Billy was his favorite.

Billy was the one who made him laugh. He made all of us laugh. He was the one who would break up whenever my father would get into one of his fits about whatever was bothering him that day. He could make my father laugh at himself. Christina and I could never do that. Mother couldn't. Billy could. Billy never let any of us take things too seriously.

Even when he was little he knew when I was unhappy, or when Christina was. He'd say, "You gotta come out and play with me. You'll feel better."

He used to make us take him hunting for his treasures. That's what he called them, his treasures. He always wanted to go digging in the woods. He was always hunting for arrowheads and beads and pot shards. He never found much but he didn't care. When he was very young, he thought everything was a treasure, every rock. He made us carry home buckets of rocks which ended up in Mother's garden in Pound Ridge. He did make good finds when he was older and I know Mother kept them. She is the real collector.

Mother collects Indian rugs and pottery, contemporary pottery, not the old pieces. I have some of them here in the townhouse. The townhouse is perfect for me, close to the freeway and an easy commute, if any commute is easy in this town, and Sherman Oaks is a nice place to live. I bought it when I was dating Karen and she helped me with the decorating. We painted all the walls different pastel colors and hung up the rugs Mother has given me over the years.

Karen had the idea of framing three of my father's field sketches, pencil drawings he had done out on the Navajo reservation when we were kids. She framed them like old masters, and people are always asking about them. They look like something from the early 1800s. There is the study of an old Navajo man, his head from different angles, then three women with studies of their hands weaving at a loom. There is also a little Navajo boy, full-body studies. Karen's idea of framing them like old art was right on the money. She was clever that way. Of course, Maureen is the professional.

Maureen has been helping me make some changes in the townhouse. We painted all the walls an off-white which she says is much better for the rugs and the art. She's been introducing me to the more avant-garde Native American artists. It was Maureen who steered me to Johnny Whitehair, the Navajo painter. He has a far more abstract view of his culture than painters like my father and his group. He combines the ancient symbols with modern expressionism. Very exciting.

Maureen and I are also interested in contemporary European art and we have been watching the galleries for works that fall into my price range. I did buy a good piece by a Spanish artist whose works have a batik quality about them and usually involve a single woman with a flower. I am now looking at a marble sculpture by a young Latino artist Maureen knows through her job at the design studio. I am not sure how I feel about the piece. It is a madonna type of woman, all round, curled into herself. Maureen says it has a Diego Rivera quality and would be a good investment. Perhaps, but I don't find it very attractive. It seems almost malformed to me. We'll see.

I do prefer the more abstract to my father's type of art, that picture-perfect realism for which his group is known. I was waiting for Maureen in a gallery recently when a telephone man who was working there started talking about the art. He said, "It's all right, but I like pictures that look like the real thing. That takes talent." I told him he would like my father's work and he probably would.

Maureen thinks we should have one of my father's newer pieces in the townhouse. There is no way I could buy one but she thinks Father might loan me one or give me one as a gift. Frankly, I'm a little surprised she likes his kind of art.

Gloria never liked my father's work. She never said that right out but she did say she didn't understand the point of painting things or events that never happened or had never been seen or recorded and then acting as though it was history. I remember when she found out how much my father's paintings were going for back when they were still fifty or sixty thousand. She yelled about that. I can just imagine what she'd say if she heard that he was just offered two hundred and fifty thousand for the three-panel Battle of the Little Big Horn, and it's not finished yet. Oh, would she yell.

But Gloria would laugh about the stories my father tells about how the Japanese and Germans are going crazy for anything about the old West, including his paintings. He told me they have camps in Germany were men go and play cowboys and Indians. He says they dress up and have gun battles and rope cows. Gloria would love that.

I've asked her to come out and visit, to stay with me or at least call when she's in town. She never has. She always had some smart remark to make about L.A. It isn't as though she never lived here. She lived at the beach for at least two years. Now she's in Dallas. What's so great about Dallas? From what I've seen, it operates like a cow town and takes pride in being one. The weather can be miserable, rainy, humid. I don't know why she stays there. I don't even know why she moved there.

We should have screwed that night in Mexico. Fuck Paul. That's what we should have done. Then this would all be over and done with. How could she not remember that night? She was definitely responding until she took that goddamn bottle of champagne and left. She was saving it for Paul, for all the good that did her. Paul was holding her back that night, her feelings for him. I told her it would be all right if she stayed, that he would never know, that we both needed to be with somebody on New Year's Eve. I said we were both lonely and it would be fun. I tried everything, like any guy would, to keep her there. I wanted to get laid.

I'd like to do it right here in the townhouse. We could have dinner here, the way I used to cook in Mexico. We'd have a good steak, a good bottle of wine, brandy by the fire and then we would do what we should have done twenty years ago. I get hard thinking about that, unbuttoning her blouse, unhooking her bra, feeling her nipples. Once inside her I'd stay for as long as I could, stay without moving. She has that beautiful hair and those long legs and I'd hold onto her hair with one hand and hold her still with the other. I even fantasize how I'd leave the bed when we finish. I'd walk around smoking a cigarette, look out the window. The stupid thing is I've smoked a total of two cigarettes in my life and that was over twenty years ago in Mexico.

She would be in my bed, the comforter pulled up over her breasts and all that beautiful hair falling over her shoulders and she'd be watching me. And then? Then it would be over and we'd be friends again. That's the end of the fantasy.

We could never be more than friends. Our values are too different. We always wanted different things out of life. She wants this freedom to do whatever she feels she wants to do. That's a false sense of freedom. You need money to do exactly what you want to do and she doesn't have much.

She refuses to get a real job. What is going to happen to her in ten years? Who does she have to take care of her? That's not freedom.

I'm more free than she is. I am doing exactly what I want to do, whether she believes it or not. My life isn't boring and I don't think I'm a boring person. Yes, it does hurt to be told that, even when you know it's not true. When you are feeling bad about things, you almost believe it. But I have a great life. I don't have to jump out of planes or dive off a bridge with bungee cords wrapped around my legs or go white water rafting every vacation.

You have to grow up sometime. That's what Barbara didn't understand, and Marjorie. You can't always be on the edge, running off whenever things get too rough. You have to work at life. You make a home, raise children. Yes, it may be dull at times but that's okay. The only people who can keep living life in the fast lane are race car drivers and drug addicts and they both burn out fast.

Nobody ever said I was boring in Mexico. I outdrank the best of them. I made all the trips to the whorehouses. I didn't worry about catching a disease, none of us did. It was easy enough to get treatment. You walked into a pharmacy, dropped trou' and the clerk gave you a shot of penicillin. Besides, I didn't do that again after Marjorie. I did worry about Gloria though. I think Paul went with a couple of whores when he was with her. I wondered about the risk he was putting her in. I didn't say anything. Maybe I should have, but we didn't get into each other's business down there. Besides, Paul was a player and she knew that. She should have, anyway.

She once told me she never loved him. Then why stay with him? I still don't understand that. There were a lot of other guys she could have gone with, guys who would have been good to her. Me, for one.

I have to smile when I think about how she and Paul would be in bed in the morning when I'd go in to talk. She was so relaxed about that. She would be in the bed, wearing a man's shirt, his shirt, and he'd be next to her, bare-chested, smoking a cigarette or reading a book.

It was all so innocent, nothing sexual about it. It was as though we were all in this together, this adventure, this life in Mexico. All that changed after Mexico, that relaxed attitude about everything. Can you imagine going into some couple's bedroom now, no matter how close you are, and sitting on their bed talking? I can't. I don't know people like that anymore. I don't know if I want to.

Joe once told me he had seen Paul in action with Gloria. He and Paul shared a bedroom before their other roommate moved out and Gloria would spend the night there. One night they must have thought Joe was sleeping because they started screwing. Joe told me how he could see her outlined against the light from the window. He told me it was kind of pretty, the way she was up there riding Paul, that's how he put it. I bet it was.

She was so pretty then. You have to realize that when I'd go into the bedroom she would just be getting up. She'd have no makeup on, her hair would be all over the place but she looked perfect and very, very sexy.

I still look at attractive women and wonder what they look like in the morning in bed and what they would look like making love. I wonder if they are the kind who have to grab a sheet to cover themselves when they get out of bed or whether they don't kiss you in the morning because they are worried about their breath. I do know what Gloria looked like in the morning and I have also thought about what she would look like making love and when she comes.

This is a typical thing men do, turning every woman into something sexual even when they are friends. And Gloria has been a good friend. She was the one who helped me put things into perspective when Marjorie left and when I was going through the divorce. I needed a woman to explain to me how a woman could be with you for seven years and then one day decide it's all over and you have to get out of your own house. But, like Gloria said, when a woman reaches that point, it's over. They really believe they've already done everything possible and somehow you've missed it. Maybe so, but Barbara could have talked to me first, shared her feelings with me. I deserved that much.

I'm the kind of guy who believes there is always a chance for things to work out. I told her that. I told her I didn't care about Dan Green, that we could forget that. I wanted to stay in my house with her and Ashley. That was my life. She took my life away from me. I was expected to go out and start all over again while she just went merrily on her way. Now I hear she and Allen are in counseling together. Isn't that nice. She wouldn't go to counseling to save our marriage but she'll go with somebody who isn't her husband.

She tells me everything is fine between them, that the counseling is to help them build their communication skills. What the hell is that? I should have told her to take a camping trip with Dan Green. That certainly helped her communicate her feelings to me.

I try to check on our house whenever I am up in San Francisco. It isn't blue anymore. The new owners have painted it a light yellow color. The color is all right but I miss the blue. The roses are still blooming along the fence. That makes me sad in a way. The whole thing does. We were happy there. I know that. We were happy fixing up the house together. We were happy the day we tested the blue paint on one side and decided even if it was a crazy color, we were going to do it blue.

There were good times in that house, and good feelings. We used to lay in front of the fire fireplace and make love. I know I was happy in that house. Barbara was the one who changed.

22

My father used to introduce me as his yuppie son. I suppose I did fit the bill back in the '80s, a lawyer with a house in the suburbs, wife, family and the silver Volvo.

Gloria laughed when she saw it. "Wouldn't you know," she said, "a Volvo." Yes, Gloria, a Volvo, and I've got a Mercedes now.

That is one thing that was always hard to take about her, that kind of put-down. She had something to say about everybody's life. She was always good at making you feel like what you were doing, the way you were living, was silly. Gloria acts like there is something wrong with earning a good living, making money and buying things for yourself. There's the liberal again.

People like Gloria don't understand that things like good cars, homes, art, give you pleasure. You've earned them and it's the quality that matters, not the cost. They are symbols of your position and your success. Someone in my line of work is judged by the car he drives and the way he lives. My Japanese clients don't come into town and rent a Ford. They want a Mercedes or a Lexus and they expect their lawyer to be driving a good car, not flashy, but expensive. If your lawyer isn't doing well, why would you trust him with your business? Gloria might not have to deal with that kind of reality but the rest of us do and I don't mind, not a bit.

Gloria made her choice. She could have been anything. She had it all, still does. She has the looks, the education, the brains. The last time I saw her she was driving an eight-year-old car with no air conditioning, and this is in Dallas, Texas in the summer. Her place is tiny. She has hardly any furniture. I don't think that's a good way for her to live.

Barbara used to tell me I was too concerned about Gloria, that I spent too much time thinking about her and how she lived. She always said I was in love with Gloria, whether I knew it or not. Karen said the same thing, or it might have been Linda, that she thought I was a little in love with Gloria. No, I'm not in love with her and I wasn't then.

I may still feel some of that old excitement when I think about her. She always had that effect on me. I can remember when I used to see her, it was like nobody else was in the room. I would just see her. When I'd call her my voice would get tight, like a kid with a crush. It would be like I couldn't breathe again until I saw her and we had a few drinks and started talking. But anymore, I don't want that feeling with her or anyone. I'm a little afraid of it.

The last time I saw Gloria I felt more anger than anything else. I wanted to grab her and shake her. I was so frustrated with her. There she is living from paycheck to paycheck and she still has that snotty attitude she has.

There was one time in Mexico when Paul and

I were waiting for her in the car. She came out of a store and didn't see us and she started walking. Paul was driving alongside and calling her name. Suddenly he starts yelling, "You cunt, you goddamn cunt." I said, "What the hell is wrong with you?" He said he couldn't stand the way she walked, with her nose up in the air, that attitude of hers. I was shocked then but I can understand it now. She can make you crazy.

I did think I was in love with her in Mexico. I almost told her once. It was right after Marjorie found out she was pregnant. There weren't many options back then. You either got married or had an abortion. Very few people had illegitimate children or gave their babies up for adoption. At least, I never knew anybody who did. Marjorie wasn't asking me for a decision. She said she needed to think about what she was going to do. But I had this feeling that I was going to have to make a decision for the both of us and that it could be a turning point in my life. I went over to Paul's to talk to them about what I should do.

It was one of those mornings when Gloria was still in Paul's bed. He let me in and then went off to shower. I sat on the bed and talked to her. I told her I didn't know what to do, that I was thinking about how hard it would be to go to school and be married with a kid on the way. I didn't know how I would support a child. And then there was Marjorie's art. How would she ever do that? Women didn't have children and careers back then, not many of them. Everything I had planned for my life would fall apart if we got married. Of course, I would marry Marjorie, if that's what she wanted. I told Gloria that, but it would be the end of all my dreams.

Gloria wanted to know if I was in love with Marjorie. I wasn't and I knew it. I liked her but I didn't love her. What I wanted to say to Gloria was, "No, Gloria, I don't love her, I love you." But I didn't say it. I probably said something about how much I cared for Marjorie and how I would do anything she wanted.

We didn't get into the abortion. That would be Marjorie's decision. Abortion wasn't an issue back then. We all knew people who had them. It was relatively safe down there and you could easily get the name of a doctor. Of course, I don't feel that way now. Now the thought of destroying a baby makes me sick, but back then we didn't think of it that way. In the end, Marjorie had the abortion. That's what she wanted.

But that's when I should have told Gloria how I felt about her. I was going on and on about all the pros and cons of marrying Marjorie but what I was really trying to do was to get her to say, "Don't marry her, Andrew. Marry me. I'm the one you should marry." That's what I wanted her to say and if she had said one word, shown any sign at all that she didn't want me to marry Marjorie, I would have told her how I felt. I would have told her we were the ones who should get married. Forget Marjorie.

I would have done it, too. I would have kissed off Dartmouth. I would have changed my whole life from that minute on. I would have dragged her out of that bed and down to whatever person could marry us in that town. But, as usual, Gloria acted like none of it mattered, me, Marjorie, the baby, nothing.

Just as well. I needed to get out of there. I needed to get into a real college. I also needed to get away from Gloria and whatever it was she was doing with Paul. Oh, it might have been exciting to stay with her for awhile. She was always good for putting some excitement in life. She is still telling me to go out and have an adventure. That's what she says. "Had any adventures lately, Andrew?" I've had my adventures, thank you, and they haven't been much fun.

That day in Mexico was an adventure. That walk down the road with those men, that was a real adventure. I can remember telling myself not to walk too fast, to look relaxed, like I had all the time in the world. I was looking straight ahead. I didn't look at the men around us. That was important.

At first it wasn't that bad. They were along the sides of the road, not following us. Gloria says they were like animals, cow-like, passive. She says they swayed as we walked past. I don't know about that, but I remember thinking even then that the situation looked like it could get bad, real bad. I was thinking that this is how revolutions get started, that all they needed was for someone to start yelling, telling them what to do, and they'd break loose and start destroying everything in sight.

They weren't crazy or drunk and not that angry at first. At first it was mostly the kids who were following us. They were laughing at us, a little pushing, that was all. Then the bastards moved in.

They were yelling, "Guera, guera," at Gloria. "Blond girl, blond girl." To them any light-haired American girl was a guera. They used to yell it at the girls when they were walking down the streets even when one of us was with them.

By this time it was moving into a riot situation. The priest was on the loudspeaker trying to keep them calm but who could hear him? There was so much noise, all those people. We could hardly walk forward with all the people around us. Paul was in front, then Gloria, and me behind her. I was hit at least once. I was punched hard on my back. I was waiting for the knife to slide in between my ribs. It was a long way down that road, I can tell you that.

Paul was as scared as I was. I know that because when we were finally back in the car he yelled at Gloria. He said it was all her fault, that she had gotten us into this. He had to have been scared shitless to turn on her like that, really yelling at her. But it wasn't her fault. It wasn't anybody's fault.

This was riot, pure and simple, and it didn't have anything to do with us. I can remember a girl screaming at one point, a Mexican girl. She was up against a wall and her blouse was ripped. The blouse was pink and it was hanging down from one shoulder. She was trying to cover herself. Glass was breaking around us. I remember gunshots and men running in the street. That's when we fell into the church. We were flat up against this wall where the girl was, and then suddenly we fell through the doors of this church. That's the way it seemed. We wouldn't have gotten there at all if it hadn't been for Gloria. She was the one who kept yelling, "To the church. We have to get to the church."

I don't think she was actually yelling, "Sanctuary, sanctuary," like the hunchback of Notre Dame, but she knew what she was doing. The church was the one place we would be safe. She knew that because she was Catholic and so were the Mexicans.

Sometimes I tell myself it couldn't have been that bad, that Gloria must be exaggerating about that day, that we've both blown it way out of proportion because we were young. But if it wasn't that bad why did we end up fighting our way to the church. If it wasn't that bad we would have walked to the car and driven back to the city. And I do remember that girl in the pink blouse. They must have been raping her or had tried to rape her. We were damn lucky to make it to that church. Paul should have known that. Gloria wasn't at fault. She saved us.

I suppose all riots start like that, a party, a good time, people laughing, enjoying themselves. Then something happens, something goes wrong and everything changes. That's what happened that day. It turned into a riot. Not because we were Americans, Gloria is wrong about that. Mexicans like Americans, as a rule.

Nothing changed for me because of that day. Linda was wrong about that, thinking it would have changed her whole life, the way she looked at life. No. We all went on as planned. Marjorie and I went to Chicago, Becks and Joe went up to Dallas, and Paul and Gloria went to his mother's in Tennessee.

I was ready. I wanted to get back to America and Americans. Mexico was so frustrating. Everything was a problem. You couldn't make a phone call without a hassle, or the water would be turned off for no reason, or the lights would go off for hours. Something was always wrong and you were supposed to accept it. You would go crazy if you didn't. After a while, all any of us wanted to do was go back to the States.

One of the things we missed the most was American food. Becks would make great fried chicken for us with mashed potatoes and a big salad. We ate American as a rule. You can't eat tacos all the time and the food wasn't all that good. The best vegetables and fruits were exported to the States and the meat was terrible, tough, stringy. When we'd be driving to 'pulco Paul would point to the Mexican cows and say, "That's why the steaks are so tough." The cows did look like they were starving but the people didn't have much to eat either.

Paul was one of the guys who didn't like the Mexicans. As bad as he was sometimes about them, he could make you laugh. One time we were riding down the Reforma in Joe's car. We were at a stoplight and Paul starts pointing to a guy standing on the corner, saying, "Look, he's wearing plastic wingtips."

We all started looking at the guy. He was wearing a cheap suit and his shoes did look like they were plastic. We start laughing. Joe was laughing so hard he almost crashed the car when the light changed. It was cruel. I know that. I knew it then. The guy must have known we were laughing at him. But we were young and we got into this American thing, always hanging around with other Americans. I think it was because we felt outnumbered.

I never learned the language. I feel bad about that. I learned enough to buy groceries and to get around. Languages have always been hard for me. Paul and Gloria spoke it the best. They would translate for the rest of us. After awhile, we all depended on Gloria, Paul included. We were lazy.

She'd talk to the maid and do the shopping. One time she went out with Terry Seiffert to get his car fixed. When they got back Terry told us how some kid in the street came up and tried to sell him his sister, then his brother, then his mother, and finally himself and Gloria is standing right in the middle doing all the translating.

I think Paul's feelings about the Mexicans were probably due to where he was raised, Tennessee. Joe was from a typical blue collar family in the Midwest and there's a lot of prejudice up there. I saw that when I was in Chicago. But Gloria was never cruel about them and I didn't mean to be.

I never told anybody this but I wanted to make a difference down there. I had read *The Ugly American* while I was at Choate and it made a real impression on me. I wanted to change the way Americans were seen in the world. I actually thought about a career in the State Department for awhile. I thought I could go in after law school. I certainly had no prejudice against anyone or any country. I wanted to make a difference.

I would have liked to have known more Mexicans. I would have liked to date a Mexican girl. But they didn't make it easy. They didn't like that. Not the men anyway. It was okay for them to date our women but not okay for us to date the Mexican girls. I don't think an American would have made it down a street with a Mexican girl. Not at night, anyway. Whose fault is that?

I could never get past the stealing. Everybody stole, not just the poor. The maid stole, no matter how much you paid her. They'd steal your dirty laundry. A piece would always be missing when the maid brought it back. They took things out of your mail. You were always being ripped off and it made a lot of us mad because we didn't understand why they did it. I met one guy down there who told me how he would put a stereo in the back seat of his car. Then he would sit up in the window of his apartment with a rifle. He'd sit up there watching as these guys would circle the car, looking around to see if anybody was watching. Then they'd reach for the car door and he'd yell. They'd look up and he would be up there aiming right at them. He wasn't going to shoot. He said he just wanted to scare the shit out of them. He said at least the ones he caught wouldn't be back.

There was a story about a group of ex-marines down there who had come up with a list of how much they thought the Mexicans owed them. They added up the bribes, everything that had been stolen, checks they never got. Then they went out and systematically broke up clubs and skipped out on restaurant bills. They would estimate how much damage they were going to cause that night to repay one of their losses. They would make a planned assault and the minute they thought they had recouped their loss, they left. No, I didn't approve but I did understand their frustration.

Overall, I know the Mexicans were good people. They were good to us. They put up with a lot from us. We were rowdy. We drank too much, partied all the time. We could be really obnoxious, and we all had so much money to spend and they had so little.

People like Gloria always say the rest of the world hates us because of the way we act. I don't see that. I think it's more jealousy than hate. They want what we have, our music, our movies, our blue jeans. They idolize American women. I saw that in Mexico. They didn't hate us, the Mexicans. And if they did, that makes me sad because I liked them, I really did.

Maybe it was a mistake to spend most of my time down there with other Americans but it was only natural. You go to your own. The Americans I knew, my friends, were great. I still think about them twenty-five years later. We formed a bond down there. We felt safe with one another. When Mexico got too much for us, we could always get back to our American reality. That's how we could have a party after that day. We needed a party. We needed to feel American again.

We were all fine by the time we got to Paul's.

I had calmed down in the church. Once we got in there everything was okay, like all the things that had gone on outside were finished. We were safe in there, that's how I felt. Gloria said we could get a priest if there was any trouble but I knew there wasn't going to be any. Paul was angry at that point. Gloria and I were sitting together but he moved down the pew away from us. His jaw was tight and he was making kind of a snorting noise. He did blame her.

We must have been in the church close to an hour, just sitting. There was one other person in there, an old Mexican lady with a shawl, a rebozo, over her head. She had lit a candle and was kneeling before one of the statues. Gloria had something on her head too, a scarf. That's how careful she had been. She wanted to show them that she respected their religion. She hadn't come for any kind of a show. None of us had. I can still see the light in that church, all the candles flickering, and the golden light all around us like a haze. That light was so pretty. I felt totally relaxed, like I could breathe again. I felt like I had come home.

I've heard people say that, how they had come into some situation that made them feel as though they had finally come home. They are usually talking about meeting the right person or finding Christ. But, for me, I think I felt that in that church, being totally at peace. I think I could have stayed there the rest of my life. Then we left and went back to the car.

All I remember about that is how normal everything was. There were no crowds in the streets, no riots. It was as though the whole thing had been a bad dream, like none of it had really happened. My car was fine and we drove back to the city. But O'Brien's tires had been slashed, all four of them, not just flat. I had forgotten that.

That's what he told us when he finally got to the party. They had slashed his tires. The poor guy. The only thing he ever did to the Mexicans was drink a lot of their beer.

23

I haven't asked Maureen to marry me in the official sense. We've discussed our feelings about marriage and children but there is no need to rush. Let's see how things work out. We have time. That's how I feel. I don't want to make another mistake although I doubt I would be with Maureen. We have so much in common. But I couldn't handle another divorce. I've had my fill of women who find themselves by leaving me. Not that Maureen is like that. She isn't. She understands that I am happy right now with how things are going and she isn't the kind of woman who would push a man into doing something he wasn't ready to do.

There was a time when I might have talked to Gloria about something like this, get a woman's opinion. But it's been a while since we've talked. The last time I called her it was uncomfortable. I felt like I had to keep talking, telling her things to keep her interested. I also feel like I have to watch what I say around her. There are so many things going on in my life she wouldn't understand.

I do feel that my life has a purpose. I believe God has a plan for me. That belief has given me stability in my life. Share that with Gloria? I don't think so. And that's where friendship ends, when you can't share what makes you happy. Besides, Maureen and I share so much I don't need to talk to

Gloria the way I used to.

She's too negative. She thinks she sees everything so clearly but she doesn't. Most of what she sees, what she talks about, is very negative. For example, the last time we talked I mentioned Ken Wilmont, a guy we knew in Mexico. I was wondering what happened to him. He used to talk about studying for the ministry and I wondered if he ever made it. Gloria said he was probably dead from AIDS. I asked her why she said that and she said Ken Wilmont was gay, everybody knew that. Didn't I know that? No, I didn't, and I don't know that it's true now. Why can't I be allowed to remember the guy the way I want to? Why does she always have to be the truth teller? I don't need that negativity in my life.

Even the sexual excitement I always felt around her has a dark side to it. Something happened down there that I've never talked about. It was after the party at Paul's. I saw something going on between him and Gloria.

He was mad at her on the ride back to the city but everything was okay by the time we got to the apartment. I saw him kissing her in the kitchen, a real long passionate kiss. He did like her even if he would never admit it to any of us. But that isn't what I saw.

After awhile, I got tired of the noise and the smoke and I needed to get some air so I went up on the roof. The other guys were trying to get up a trip to Garibaldi to hear the mariachis but I had had about enough for one day.

All the apartments in Paul's building were

on a central air shaft. Either a bedroom or the kitchen window opened on to it. When I was up there I realized you could look down the shaft right into some of the apartments. I didn't know that. I had only been up there those times for the newly-weds. Paul's apartment was on the top floor, so standing on the roof I could see right into his bedroom. The curtains were wide open that night.

I still get sick thinking about what happened up there. I saw Paul and Gloria on his bed. She was kneeling over him, giving him a blow job. He had his hands on her head, wrapped in her hair and he was really getting off. I should have stopped watching but I didn't. I couldn't. Everything was happening so fast.

When they were finished he jumped off the bed and walked over to the window. He was wiping himself off with something, a tissue. He had jumped out of the bed so fast I didn't have time to step back. I swear right before he turned off the light on the desk, he looked up like he knew somebody was up there watching. He had to know you could see into the bedroom. He had been up on that roof often enough. Just like with Joe watching them do it. That son of a bitch had to know.

Gloria was sitting there. All she was wearing were her panties. She was not smiling or anything. That's why I missed him getting up so fast. I was watching Gloria.

The whole thing made me sick. Still does. Her doing that and the way he looked up, almost smiling. Why did I have to see that? It made me sad in a way, but it also made me sick. I was drunk, the whole day had been a mess, and now him probably catching me watching them. What the hell would he think of me? I threw up right there, puked my guts out. I was trying to be quiet but I was thinking, Great, Paul probably sees me watching them fuck and then he comes up here and finds a pile of puke.

I must have been crazy but I started running back and forth carrying water in my hands from the basins where the maids washed the clothes. I was trying to wash the puke away and I was scared to death somebody was going to come up there and see me. When I got as much of it off as I could, I looked back over the edge for a second and saw that Paul's curtains were closed. Now they were closed. He knew exactly what he was doing.

That night I had to walk for a long time before I found a cab. The next day Frank Coppola and Terry Seiffert and I decided to take a bus to Oaxaca. It was Easter break. We had a great time down there and went to all the ruins.

I know I shouldn't feel bad about the thing on the roof. That was an accident. I didn't plan it. I wasn't a Peeping Tom. That was Paul, not me. I doubt he saw me. If he did know somebody was up there, he didn't know it was me. The other thing is, in a way it was a turn-on. Any man who says he doesn't get turned on by watching other people do it is lying. It's normal. I've had my fantasies about Gloria and me together, her down on her knees like she was that night. But anymore, I don't think that's healthy.

Gloria makes me nervous. Talk to her and you feel like she is inside you, like she is walking around in your brain. You don't feel like you can get away, that you could hide from her if you had to. I don't always want to. Part of me does want to run away from Gloria, but part of me always wants to go toward her.

The last time I saw her, she was still acting like a twenty-year-old, like she had her whole life in front of her. She acts as though she has all the time left to do whatever it is she wants to do. When you are with her for a few hours it starts to rub off. She gives you the feeling that everything is possible, that you could change your life in one second, fly off somewhere, move, never have to explain anything you do to anybody. For awhile, it sounds okay, especially if you are drinking, but I always felt if you ever gave in to Gloria, let loose all the way with her, you would lose control over your life. From that point on it would be you and her and no one else. You'd have to close the door on the outside world and everyone you knew. That is not a safe place to be.

Sure, I've played around with the fantasy of going away with her for a short trip, letting go for a few days. Why not? I've thought about calling her and saying, "Hey, let's go on a trip together for a week or two."

I know exactly where I'd take her. I'd take her on the train to Mexico. We'd screw our way across the desert. We'd stop at all the little towns and buys tacos and beers but mostly we'd screw. And what does she do? She tells me she is going to take a train to Mexico by herself. Stupid. That's why I got so angry. I wanted to take her on that train.

That was my dream. She'd rather go alone.

You know, I would have married her if she'd been the one who was pregnant. No question about it. There would have been no talking about an abortion. She's not the type. We wouldn't have lived together either. We would have gotten married and we would have stayed in Mexico. I could have finished school and gotten something with one of the big multinational corporations down there. I could have learned Spanish. I think we would still be together if we had gotten married. We would have been happy. I would have been and that's what Gloria has always needed, to settle down with someone who would take care of her.

All she had to do was say, "Don't marry Marjorie. I'm the one who loves you. Marry me." And she says she doesn't remember New Year's Eve. She is lying. She has to be. I remember every goddamn second of that night.

We would have been happy in Mexico. I loved that country. I liked everything about it. There are times when all I want to do is be back there. I want to hear all the people laughing and yelling and hear the car horns honking. I even liked the way it smelled. It was so full of life. I want to be back there going to a party with the guys, walking to the movies with Gloria. Those were the best goddamn times I ever had in my life. I know that.

Everything isn't perfect in my life now and I sometimes wonder why I have to act as though it is. Barbara gets on the phone about Ashley. She crabs about whatever she wants me to do about some situation she has created herself. Mother calls about my father and some problem he's having, some snit he's in. I'll be sitting in the middle of another goddamn traffic jam with some truck in front of me blowing smoke everywhere and some client will be on the phone screaming about a problem he thinks should be the most important thing in my life and I think, What the hell am I doing here? What the hell has happened to the life I wanted to live? That's when I think about going back.

There are times when I want to call Gloria and say, "Let's get the fuck out of here right now." There are times when I feel if I don't do something soon, right away, make a major change, I will never be happy again, not the way I was down there. Crazy, isn't it, to feel that way when so much of my life is so good.

I do wonder though how good my photography really was. Maybe I did have the eye. Maybe I could have been good enough to have stayed down there shooting pictures for magazines in the States, tourist shots, maybe news. Who knows? I just needed the experience, but you pick that up. If I had stayed down there, Gloria and I could have worked together. She could have written the stories while I took the pictures. Other people have done it. They've made a living that way.

You know, if I said it to her right now, if I said, "Look, Gloria, I want to get a good camera, maybe my old one, and head back to Mexico to see if I have what it takes before it's too late," she'd say "Go for it, Andrew. Have an adventure." That's exactly what she'd say.

She'd say, "What do you have to lose?"

Oh, she'd do it. Gloria would do it in a minute, go for the dream. She wouldn't feel like she had anything to lose. But I do. I have a lot to lose. Damn her.

24

Father isn't doing too well right now. His eyes have been bothering him and Mother says the doctors in Phoenix think it may have to do with the years he spent around oil paint and turpentine, all the paint he has splattered in his eyes and the fumes. They are not saying he is going blind, nothing like that, but they are worried about the deterioration he has already suffered. Right now he is trying to work out an air filtering system for his studio. He is still painting, of course. That's what he does. This must be very frightening for him, but he hasn't said much about it and Mother says there is no reason to worry yet.

I used to wonder how she could put up with him. He could be so vicious when he was angry, especially when he knew he was wrong. Oh, he can charm people. I've seen him charm my dates and friends and the people at his shows, but disagree with him, interrupt him at work, and he can lash out. He used to lash out at Mother. He'd yell, "Sarah, this has nothing to do with you. Be quiet, Sarah." I've heard him tell her to shut up, that she didn't know what she was talking about. He can be very insulting but I never heard her answer him back, not once. Maybe she did when they were alone. I kind of doubt it.

The way he treated her bothered me, especially when I was young. I would try to joke with her after he said something particularly mean. I'd try to get him on to something else. That's what Billy was doing when he tried to make us laugh, redirecting Father's attention. But as I get older I do see that the relationship works for them. She has her volunteer work and her women's groups. They have friends in Sedona and they drive into Phoenix to see shows and shop. They have a good life together. My father is also mellowing a bit. He isn't so fast to yell if you disagree with him. It isn't the relationship I would want but they will have been together for fifty years this June and that, in itself, is quite an accomplishment.

The real trick to it all is to keep growing, emotionally and professionally. I think I'm doing that. Right now I am thinking about taking classes in Japanese. Maureen wants to take them too. We are planning a two-week trip to Japan later this year and it would be great to speak a little of the language. People appreciate that, when Americans try to speak their language. They take it as a compliment. We are really looking forward to the trip.

I am moving forward with my life, doing new things, meeting new people. I don't hang on to the past like those people who keep talking about their high school days or the guys who go on and on about what their ex-wives did to them. That's not healthy.

Meeting Maureen helped me finally get past my anger about Barbara and the divorce. Now I can see the good things about Barbara. She is a good mother. She does the best she can and Ashley is her first priority. I've stopped blaming her for what happened to us. I made mistakes. I should have been more aware of what was going on with her.

I still care for her, of course. Maureen knows that and she understands. She says its normal that I worry about what Barbara is doing and some of the mistakes I think she might be making. Our relationship now is based totally on doing the right thing for Ashley. I pay my child support without a complaint. Maureen was shocked when she found out how much I was paying. She said most fathers would fight paying that kind of money and nobody would let his ex-wife keep all the profits from the sale of the house they bought together. I suppose that's true. But I did what I thought was fair for Ashley and Barbara regardless of what she did to me.

We've been going around and around on Ashley's education. I think private-school education is invaluable. Even now when I meet a man who prepped at one of the good Eastern schools, there is an immediate bond. You need that bond today. You need every edge you can get. I don't know how important it is for a girl as young as Ashley, but it is something to think about. Barbara has never been hot on private schools until recently. Now she is taking about Ashley going into a parochial school. I have some reservations about that, especially because of the amount of religious indoctrination that may go on in those schools. But, the education level is high. I wonder how Allen likes the idea. If he ever marries Barbara, his step-daughter would be going to a Catholic school, and he's Jewish. However he feels about it, Barbara will get her way. She always does.

I wonder how Barbara would feel if she knew I was considering marriage again. Maureen says ex-wives often get upset when their husbands remarry, no matter how long they've been divorced. She says they get jealous, especially if they haven't remarried first. They still like to think you are there for them should they ever want you back again. I doubt Barbara would feel like that. She'd probably laugh and wish me luck. Of course, you never know. Could be interesting

Maureen wants to have a family while she is still young enough. I've thought about that. I could do that, be a father again. Men in their forties and fifties are having children all the time in this country. We are so much younger now than our fathers were at this age. Ashley would like a little brother or sister and with Maureen staying at home, she could come down more often and stay longer. Maureen adores Ashley and that makes me happy.

I think Grandfather would approve of what I've done with my life. Maybe I didn't make it through Dartmouth but we all can't be Dartmouth grads or dedicate our lives to defending the innocent, or the guilty, for that matter. And I did choose law, even if it was tax law. He liked that.

He used to say, "Get those sons of bitches any way you can, Andy." He meant the government. Of course, I don't do that. I make the system work for the client. I am not at war with the government.

Grandfather was a Roosevelt Democrat. Watergate almost destroyed him. He used to yell,

"Hang the bastards by their balls. Let them swing in the wind." He meant Nixon and Ehrlichman and Haldeman, all of them. They were lawyers, you see, and Grandfather believed the whole country would despise the legal profession because of what they had done, or what he thought they had done. But I still see respect for my profession. We are needed. We protect the interests of the individual, protect their rights. I am not ashamed of what I do. I do a good job. That's all they can ask of you, to do your best. I am honest, I work within the law. I have tried to be a good husband and a father. I have no regrets about my life.

There was a time when I thought about going into politics. I thought I might finish up at Dartmouth, get my law degree and then run for public office. That concept of changing the world again. I even thought about joining the Peace Corps, going into some village and working with the people. Not very realistic, I know. What those people need down there are farmers and teachers, not lawyers. But there was a time when I thought about it.

I can do my part right here. I may not be able to change the world the way a twenty-year-old thinks he can but I can make a difference. I make myself available for seminars on real estate taxation for small investors, and I sometimes do it for free or for a small honorarium. I've thought about teaching a class at one of the junior colleges and that certainly wouldn't be for the money. There isn't any. Our firm doesn't do pro bono work per se but I am always willing to take a client's financial situation into consideration in the billing. I suppose there may be some legal-aid type of work I could do if I ever had any time free from the case load at the office. And I do work for the church. I do my part.

I look at the future as being very positive. In a few years I may be married with a new child. I may not even be in L.A. Maureen and I have talked about how nice it would be to live in a small town, the kind of place where you would want to raise a family, but I'm not sure I want to leave this area. Not now, anyway.

She's right, though. You do have to consider what's going on here if you have children. Public schools are battlegrounds. The crime and the violence are out of control. They are selling drugs to kids in first and second grades. A lot of it is in the inner city but we're seeing it everywhere and a great deal of it has to do with the Hispanic population. You can't read a newspaper in this part of the country without seeing how many crimes involve someone with a Hispanic surname and many of them are illegals. That's not prejudice, that's reality. We are being overwhelmed. Our schools are falling apart, our hospitals, the entire social service system.

Some people out here believe it's all over, that there is no hope. They are leaving the area. They are going north to Oregon or Washington or over to Nevada and Arizona. Maureen knows people who are moving back to the East Coast. I hate to think I might have to leave a city I love because our government won't deal with the repercussions of illegal immigration.

Of course, any change I make includes Ashley. I want to stay relatively close to her. As it is, I am not able to get up to San Francisco as often as I would like, and I think she is still too young to come down by herself. I know Maureen is right when she says as Ashley gets older she'll want to spend more and more time with her friends and less time with her old dad, so making a move wouldn't be out of the question. No matter where we live, Ashley will always be able to come out for the summer.

I'm a lucky man in a lot of respects. I know in my heart that I am where I should be. I have a good job, good friends. I like the steady life. I don't mind putting on the suit and tie and heading into the office every morning. A lot of people complain about the time they have to spend on the freeways but I turn on the cds and drink my coffee and watch the other drivers. I'm fine.

Everyone, every man, gets frustrated with his life at some point and gets the idea that he should change it all in one fell swoop, start all over somewhere else. Not me. I may make some changes in my life but they won't be catastrophic. They don't have to be. Maureen says she is happy to hear it, that she has seen enough changes in her life already. I had to laugh. How many changes could a twenty-six-year-old girl have gone through? Still, look what I had done by the time I was twenty-six.

When you get right down to it, I can't think of a single thing I would have done differently. Not considering the circumstances at the time. Not even the abortion. What could I have done? Marjorie made the decision. I would have married her if that's what she wanted. There were a lot of screwy things that happened down there but I wouldn't have done anything differently.

Sometimes I wonder if Gloria remembers that man's hand, the way it hung off the stretcher, the way it bounced along the ground. That was bad. His hand was bouncing along the ground as they came down the hill. Wouldn't he have to be dead to have that happen, to let his hand bounce like that? There is something else and I've never been sure if it wasn't part of some dream. I remember seeing blood on that hand, or I dreamed I saw blood. Gloria never mentions it. Maybe she didn't see it or maybe it wasn't there. But I saw Paul go over to the grass after the stretcher was gone. He was bending over and looking at something on the grass. Then he rubbed his shoe on it. Was it blood? Is that what he was rubbing at?

And what happened to that man carrying the stretcher, the one I remember so well? How did he end up on my side both going up the hill and coming down? Did they have to pull the nails out, those soldiers? Somebody had to. Did that guy have to or did he have to watch somebody else do it? That must have been awful for him.

What could I have done that day? What could any of us have done? Maybe we didn't belong there but we didn't know that when we went out there. It wasn't our fault. We didn't know what was going to happen. If those people had wanted to kill us, there was nothing we could have done. Nothing. If they had gone for Paul or Gloria, I would have had to watch. I couldn't have fought them off. I never felt safe in Mexico after that day, not for one minute, except for that time in the church.

But I don't think about it anymore. I don't talk about it. I've never told Maureen about it. She would understand how I felt that day, but why would I tell her? It was such a negative experience. We share almost everything but there are some things you should keep to yourself. There are also things you should try to forget. What good does it do to remember? Besides, maybe that man didn't die at all. There's always that possibility.

I won't talk about that day again. I never did except when Gloria was around. I doubt I could even tell the story without her because I am not really sure what happened that day. I am not so sure she is either.

The other day my father asked about her. He said, "What ever happened to that little hippy girl, Andrew? Do you ever see that little hippy friend of yours?" Then he said, and this made me laugh, "You know, I always liked that gal. She was a great talker."

Yes, I guess she was. She also was a great kisser. I remember that. Kissing Gloria was like eating chocolate. That's the way it was that night, like eating chocolate candy and then licking your lips. I could have kissed her forever. As crazy as she can be, like being stuck in the middle of a lightning storm, there was always something calming about Gloria.

I felt it that night in my apartment and when

we were upstairs at the party and she was sitting at my feet. I have felt that way in Sedona. After everyone has gone to bed, I've felt that calm again, knowing she was there, even though I was still thinking about how I'd like to go into her room and get in bed with her. Sometimes there is a peace about being with Gloria that I don't understand but I like it when it's there.

Sure, I've had those thoughts about what it would be like to quit, sell everything and walk away. I have thought about it, how I could cash in and leave a lump sum for Ashley and her education. Then I would head back down to Mexico where the living is cheap. That's as far as it goes. I can get a little shaky, thinking like that, thinking about running away, because I wonder how much I do want that kind of life again. Could I really live every day like it was an adventure and not worry about money and responsibilities? I don't think so. Maybe that makes me a coward, but hey, I'm getting up there. Things change as you get older.

Gloria is the brave one, she always was. That's one reason I'll always like her. She is free and full of life. I wonder how she'd react if I showed up at her place and said, "Okay, Gloria, let's cut the shit. You and me were always supposed to be together. Let's go back to Mexico. I'll find us a little town by the ocean where we can live. Or we'll stay in the city. Whatever you want. I'll take my pictures and you'll write the articles, have babies. Whatever it is you want to do."

Sometimes I have the fantasy that she'll be the one to do it. That she'll show up at my door. She'll say, "Come on, Andy, let's hit the road. Let's head out for Vera Cruz or San Miguel. Let's go and never come back."

If we did go we wouldn't come back. I know that and that's why I don't do it. To do that, to be with her, you'd have to give up everything, everything you believed in, everything you worked for. You'd have to give up your whole life. That's not what I want.

I am right where I should be, doing what I should be doing. I am feeling better about myself than I have in years. I live better than ninety-nine percent of the people on earth in the best country there is. Most of the people I know live the same way. The people I knew in Mexico built good lives for themselves. Joe and Becks are in Texas, Terry Seiffert is with a company in New Jersey. Marjorie's okay. Of course, Mike O'Brien died in Viet Nam. I think Gloria told me that. He was such a nice guy. I thought about looking for his name on the Wall when I was in Washington last summer but I didn't get around to it. Maybe next time.

I have no plans right now to go anywhere but to Japan with Maureen and to make a few visits to my parents in Sedona. I don't want to go back to Mexico and Maureen says she has no interest in ever going there, with all the poverty and the violence. She says she can see all she needs to see of Mexico down on Olvera Street.

But if I ever did go back, with or without Gloria, I know one thing I would do. I would try to find that church where we ran that day, that pretty church with all the candles and that golden light. I do want to see that church again. I think maybe if I sat in that church again, in the same pew where we sat that day, I might be able to touch on something important in my life, something about that day. Maybe I could remember if there was a choice I made that day that affected the rest of my life.

It's silly, of course. The whole damn country is filled with churches exactly like that one. I'd never find that church again, even with Gloria, if I looked forever.

Epilogue

25

I never thought I'd be back in this place but here I am. Pam talked me into it. She said it would be a good time to take a trip with Dan and Cy. She said we could fly here, spend a couple of days in the city and then take a tour down to 'pulco and fly back home from there. I don't know where she got the wild hair but it was probably more Cy than her. Still, we're here and it ain't that bad, not much different from the way it was before.

The girls are out shopping and Dan is in the bar sopping up Mexican beer. That's all he talked about the whole plane ride down, how great Mexican beer was supposed to be. I told him I drank enough of it to know that twenty-five years ago. But I have to admit, that first one we had when we got here tasted great. The Mexicans make good beer. Always did.

I brought the clipping with me. I stuck it in my wallet right before we left the house. I don't know why but I wanted to have it with me. I cut it out of the paper a few years ago. It was in the international section, only a few lines, but I saw it right away, a couple of paragraphs about the Mexican government having a problem with some squatters. They were moving into a mountain area near the city, a place called Iztapalapa. The government wanted them out because they wanted to make the whole place into an ecological zone, whatever that means.

I'm pretty sure Iztapalapa was the name of the town where they hung that guy up. We were probably on one of those mountains the Mexican government is so worried about. Now that I'm down here I am actually thinking about making a run out there tomorrow when Pam and Cy and Dan are out at the pyramids.

The reason I think it is the same place is that newspaper article Ricardo sent the year after it happened. I kept that one too. I put it away in some book or something. I looked for it when I saw this one, to check the name, but I couldn't find it.

From what I've seen of the traffic here, it will probably take five hours to get out there tomorrow. What a mess. Maybe I'll get lucky and get a cab driver who speaks some kind of English. My Spanish is gone, at least for that kind of thing.

I've also been thinking about checking out some of the old places, the apartment over on Mariano Escobedo. We had some good old times there. We used to lower a basket out of the window and have one of the boys from the market across the street fill it with food and booze and then we'd pull it back up. I wonder what happened to all the guys. Most of them were rich to begin with so they're doing good. I am sure of that.

I'm not doing so bad myself. I was right to move into real estate when I did. Business has really picked up the past few years. I also lucked out when Mary Jo agreed to the divorce settlement as easily as she did. She could have really stuck it to me but she didn't, not much, anyway. She got the kids, and the house for two years, and a little pile when the business sold. Fine by me. I like living in Memphis and I always liked the real estate end better than the insurance.

Pam is a good wife and I don't mind her kids. She makes a good salary teaching and with her vacations and me making my own hours, we have more than enough time to get away and go up to the lake. We haven't taken any long trips until this one, and I wasn't all that hot about leaving the country, but she got a smokin' good deal on the package. So here I am back in Mexico.

If I go out there tomorrow, assuming I can find a cab driver who knows where it is, really knows where it is, not just saying so, I am going to see if that church is still there. That was the weird thing. The day they hung the guy up they had bags over all the statues in the church. I think it had something to do with Easter, but man, it was strange. Big, black bags. I hadn't thought about that until right this minute. Jesus, what a place.

I don't know how these things happen to me.

Paul Monroe
Hotel Geneva
Mexico City,

April 199_

Kathleen Walker did her undergraduate work in Mexico and her graduate work at Fairfield University, Connecticut. For ten years, as a television reporter and producer, she covered the American Southwest. More recently she has worked as a freelance writer. Her first book, *San Xavier: The Spirit Endures*, was published in 1998. *A Crucifixion in Mexico* is her first novel.